Stephen Gallagher (signature)

Stephen Gallagher

This special signed edition is limited to 1000 numbered copies.

This is copy 748.

THE NEXT THING YOU SEE WHEN YOU DIE

THE NEXT THING YOU SEE WHEN YOU DIE

STEPHEN GALLAGHER

Subterranean Press 2024

The Next Thing You See When You Die
Copyright © 2024 by Stephen Gallagher.
All rights reserved.

Dust jacket illustration
Copyright © 2024 by Claudia Caranfa.
All rights reserved.

Interior design Copyright © 2024
by Desert Isle Design, LLC.
All rights reserved.

Signed, Limited Edition

ISBN
978-1-64524-209-3

Subterranean Press
PO Box 190106
Burton, MI 48519

subterraneanpress.com

Manufactured in the United States of America

That Elizabeth-Jane Farfrae be not told of my death,
or made to grieve on account of me.
& that I be not bury'd in consecrated ground
& that no sexton be asked to toll the bell
& that nobody is wished to see my dead body
& that no murners walk behind me at my funeral
& that no flours be planted on my grave
& that no man remember me.
To this I put my name.

—Thomas Hardy, *The Mayor of Casterbridge*

1

BEFORE HEADING OUT onto the floor, Rhianna checked the supplies on her cart. Dusters, washcloths, disinfectant sprays. Two fresh trash bags, one inside the other, and a checklist of the areas to cover. Womenswear first, then down to hardware. On the front of the cart were twin buckets and a squeegee and under the dusters a boxcutter for laying open the hand of anyone who tried to detain her, should her cover be blown.

Cut and run. She was young, she could move.

She rolled the cart through flap doors and out onto the sales floor. The store was in the final stages of closing, all exits but the main one secured and Gary the mall guard standing by with his keys. He was there to nod out the last of the shoppers and turn away any would-be latecomers. After rolling down the shutter he'd be looking through the cubicles and clothing racks for anyone hiding. Always made a big show of it. He was convinced that kids would be waiting to party in the empty store like they'd never heard of cameras or motion sensors.

Rhianna had noted that he also stole tried-on lingerie from the hangers in women's changing.

If it came to it, she could handle Gary.

She knew the names of some of the staff. None of them knew hers. If they asked she'd be Celie, the woman whose employment history she'd used to get the job. She'd been here since the start of the month and was good for maybe another week. By then she'd have cleaned up in more ways than one.

"I love this color," Becky was saying, bagging up the final sale of the day for a woman in slacks and a flower print blouse. Becky dropped the receipt in the store bag and handed back the woman's Visa card. The woman headed for the exit and Becky stayed just long enough to tidy the counter and log out of her terminal. Becky had places to be. She didn't even glance at the waiting Rhianna as she headed for the staff lockers backstage.

Rhianna moved in with cloth and spray. She placed herself between the counter and the camera bubble overhead. With a flourish of the cloth she hooked the card skimmer from the terminal, concealing the move with a magician's dexterity.

After her wipe down of the counter she reached under for the waste bin. When she moved on a couple of minutes later the skimmer was in the space between the trash bags on her cart, safely out of sight.

By the end of the shift she'd collected two more of the units. They were Russian-made, a perfect shell designed to fit over the store's brand of card reader. The criminal organisation that sold them provided the software and online training for their use. A skilled eye could spot them, most would not. Each chip collected up to four

THE NEXT THING YOU SEE WHEN YOU DIE

thousand swipes on a single charge. The extracted numbers would be separated into batches for sale and resale on the so-called Dark Web, a task handled by a backroom team in a Glendale strip mall. By the time the stolen numbers went into use, "Celie" would be no more and those slick little machines would be working elsewhere.

There was one reader still to get from the cafeteria, with a battery good until noon tomorrow. She'd traded hours with another of the cleaning squad, a nightbird named Evie who hated early starts. First thing in the morning, "Celie" would be punching back in. But she was done for today.

The staff locker room was a bare and functional space but the locker door gave cover to get the devices into her backpack. Then she took off the headscarf and shook out her hair, a home dye job with roots starting to show. There was a mirror screwed to the wall, and she checked herself in it. Suddenly she was a person, not some anonymous service worker. She glanced around. No one was watching.

She left the mall through the sports store. To get to the Metrolink she had to pass the Ikea and cross under the freeway. Ray would be there to meet her on the other side with another backpack for the switch, not identical but close enough. He'd spin off on his dirt bike and she'd take the train home.

And there he was. Ray was a couple of years younger, thin as a rail in his Timberland boots. They were related somehow, cousins of some kind, too many degrees of separation to work it out. His stubble was meant to add maturity, but it grew patchy. He fell into step beside her.

"They got him," he said as they traded bags.

Rhianna stopped in her tracks. Ray kept going, heading for his bike. He looked back and said, "They're moving him now. Armen said wait for a call."

IT WAS the longest wait she'd ever known. She spent an hour of it at her dressing table, getting ready. This was going to be a big night.

Hers was a cramped room in an East Hollywood apartment, billeted with an uncle and aunt she barely knew. Rhianna was sharp and she was bright, but her choices were limited and her treasures were few. She put on makeup, maybe a little too much. But it mattered because she was doing it for Nico.

Her phone vibrated just as she was drawing in an eyebrow. The message was brief, a car on its way to collect her. The VIP treatment, for one night only.

On the way out she passed her aunt, who said nothing. As she emerged from the building a Porsche SUV came into view. When it drew level she saw that they'd sent Bela to drive her. Bela was thickset, heavy, built like a nightclub doorman with little in the way of conversation.

That was fine. She wasn't looking for distraction.

The drive took twenty minutes. The strip mall businesses were mostly closed for the night, the front parking all but empty.

"Armen said to go right in," Bela told her.

There was a boy on the door. He relocked it behind her as she made her way through darkness. The storefront had been a bakery but the ovens had been cold for most of a year. Empty steel racks betrayed its original purpose. All of the action tonight was in the back room where the tech crew normally worked; the inner door opened at her knock, a sudden reveal of light and noise.

Around twenty people were crowded in there, all against the walls like they'd made a circle for a cockfight. An exclusively male gathering until Rhianna's arrival. They made a place for her as she slid in amongst them. At the centre of the circle, under the harshest of work lights, was a lone man bound to a chair.

He had not been treated kindly.

His arms were gaffer-taped behind him and his mouth was covered with a broad strip of the same. He was conscious, but he'd slumped over as far as his bonds would allow. To either side of him in the circle of light stood Moses and Raffi, each ready to push him back upright if he leaned too far. Before him stood Armen. Short, thickset, angry Armen, looking like a blue-collar manager with his necktie loosened and his shirtsleeves rolled up.

Armen was thumbing through pictures on his phone.

"What we have here," he was saying, "is the harvest of your last six years."

The man in the chair was breathing hard over the tape, panting steam like a broken whistle. Armen found what he was looking for and turned his phone around, holding the screen before the captive's eyes.

"You remember Reuben," he said. "Shot five times by the cops. Walked right into it and never had a chance."

The man in the chair lifted his gaze. He wasn't looking at the phone. He was looking straight at Armen. He was scared, for sure, but Rhianna could see defiance there. She began to edge her way through the crowd, sliding along to get into his line of sight.

Next picture.

"Pete Kricorian. Stabbed in jail. After you put him there."

No response. Another.

"Anita took her own life when her boy was convicted. Maybe she could have been stronger. Who am I to judge?"

Rhianna saw the prisoner's focus shift. He'd seen her. Armen was swiping to his fourth and final picture.

"And Nico," he said, presenting the screen. "Maybe you thought you got to Nico before he could say what he found on your phone."

No response. When Armen realised that he no longer had the man's attention he looked back over his shoulder.

He acknowledged Rhianna with a nod. She was aware but she didn't respond, didn't break her stare but held her face set, eyes burning with unshed tears.

Armen returned his attention to the man in the chair.

"Yep," he said, "it's Rhianna. All dressed up to watch you die. How does that make you feel? Nothing you want to say to her? No word for your best friend's girl?"

Raffi had moved away and was busy at the bakery's steel basins. Hard to say what he was doing because he was on the periphery of her vision. She could guess.

Armen went on, "I absolutely believed you were one of us. We all did. Don't you have any conscience—" he glanced all around. "What's his real name?"

Someone called out, "Danny."

"Do you have a conscience, Danny Undercover? Last chance to grow one. Because this is your last journey." Armen raised the phone one final time. "Remember their faces. You'll be seeing them on the other side." Then he glanced toward Raffi and motioned for him to step in.

Raffi came forward. He was holding a syringe. He moved in behind the captive's chair, and there he hesitated.

Armen said, "What?"

"I've never done one of these," Raffi admitted.

"Fuck's sake," Rhianna said, and pushed her way forward.

She took the syringe from Raffi's hand and elbowed him aside. No one moved to stop her. In one swift move she thrust the needle downward into the captive's neck and emptied the syringe contents into him. Reaction was immediate; a muffled sound like a rollercoaster scream from behind the tape. The undercover cop's entire body rose and arched against his bonds.

Rhianna put her lips close to his ear and whispered, "Sweet dreams, lover."

He kept on struggling to breathe, straining, powerless. She watched his pain develop as one might watch a flower unfolding in the rain. He fought and thrashed; eventually his eyelids began to droop and he fell back into the chair. His head fell forward. He continued to breathe in short, snorting gasps, but anyone could see that he was no longer conscious.

She slapped him a couple of times. Not hard, just to rouse him. He didn't respond.

If he wasn't in pain, she was no longer interested. Without taking her eyes off him, she moved back to join Armen.

She said, "Nico got killed for a *phone?*"

"There were two. The one we gave him, and a secret cop phone. That's the one Nico found."

Danny Undercover jerked a few times in his bonds without waking. Public pain had given way to private nightmares.

Armen raised a hand and waved toward the doors. Everyone out. Show's over.

Rhianna had a great sense of letdown. That was it? No matter how badly it went for the traitor among them, it could never be enough for her.

Armen touched her shoulder to guide her out with the others. For a gang that tried to stay below the radar, these gatherings were always a risk. Reluctantly, she began to move. Moses and Raffi would stay on to deal with the traitor cop's body when the poison had finally done with him.

"Don't worry," Armen said. "He'll suffer."

Rhianna took a last look back.

"Not enough," she said.

SHE DIDN'T sleep well. She dreamed of Nico again. As ever she could see him but he wouldn't turn, wouldn't talk to her. The way she read him, he wasn't at peace and he wanted her to know it. Such was the power of their love. People told her that Nico was gone, gone for good, and this was nothing more than her grief finding a way to express itself. It made no difference. Rhianna didn't care.

After such a restless night she overslept and had to skip the shower and catch a later train. She sat with her eyes closed for most of the ride, letting sound and motion lull her. At the mall she keyed in the numbers at the store's staff entrance and made her way down the service corridor to the locker room. She could hear voices. Normally she'd be wary, but this morning her wits were dulled.

That changed in a second.

She stopped in the doorway. In the wall mirror she could see a uniformed cop searching through her locker while her supervisor stood by with the passkey, watching alongside a second officer. Rhianna's first thought was that they'd found her last device. But the stolen card numbers weren't on the market yet, too soon for them to have been traced back to the store.

Then she heard the second officer say, *We're pulling in the whole gang today. They're busting doors all over town.*

She drew back, choosing her moment so they wouldn't catch her movement in the mirror. If they didn't know she'd traded shifts, they wouldn't be expecting her.

She left by the way she'd come in, head bowed under the camera like always. When she'd put some distance between herself and the mall she tried to call Ray, but he wasn't picking up.

What now? Her mood hadn't been great and now her anxiety was growing. As she waited for a bus that would get her to the bakery, she checked for local news on her phone. In a radio station live stream the anchor was saying *The raids are taking place in locations through Southern California in a joint operation of the FBI, the LAPD, the DEA and the Los Angeles County Sheriff's Department* and Rhianna hurriedly muted sound in case someone overheard.

On the bus she took a seat near the back and put in her earbuds before resuming the search. Scrolling one-handed she got ads, she got a traffic report, she got weather, and finally she got *assault, robbery, firearms and drug trafficking, kidnapping and extortion, bank fraud, kidnappings and murder in an operation covering four cities and involving the use of undercover officers,* all to a montage of blocked-off streets and flashing blue lights. She thought she recognised a location but then an ad for Toyota intruded and she switched to another feed to hear *Los Angeles, Miami and Denver in one of the biggest nationwide operations of its kind* over a clip of handcuffed suits being walked out of an office building to waiting cars.

One of the men was Armen.

She could hear a helicopter overhead. The bus was getting close to the bakery and traffic was backing up. The LAPD had sealed off the block and everyone on the road was being diverted. She had a ringside seat from the bus window as the scene slid by, a veritable circus of cruisers, tech support vans, media people, and cops in armour. An unmarked vehicle behind them fired off its siren to make a way through.

Over one thousand law enforcement personnel including agents working under cover, the anchor was saying.

And aloud on the bus, Rhianna said, "Fuck."

THE NEXT THING YOU SEE WHEN YOU DIE

WHILE RHIANNA was busily dumping her work ID and everything relating to her current identity, Sergeant Vince Taylor was navigating his way through lines of security around the bakery. To be more accurate he was barging through with his badge held high, calling for news of his man.

Taylor was balding, overweight, and several months past his retirement date. He'd stayed on for the sake of Daniel Kasabian, the young officer that he'd been supervising in deep undercover for the best part of six years. Six years! The very thought dismayed him. It had never been meant to go beyond two, at the most. For five of those years he'd been Danny's only point of contact outside of his constructed identity; the boy's lifeline, his confessor, his anchor in reality. Such a role could not be taken lightly. This was the day it had all been set to end, the culmination of long planning and coordination across several states and agencies.

But with hours to go, Danny had dropped out of sight. There had been one silent call from Danny's secret phone, after which it had gone offline. This created a growing sense of apprehension that Sergeant Taylor had no power to act on. He couldn't raise an alarm. Danny Kasabian was one small part in a large and complex justice machine. The machine was on the point of delivering, and would be stopped for no one.

Now Vince Taylor stood on the threshold of the bakery's back room. Despite being stoked with dread, he knew better than to enter or touch. The crime scene people were doing their jobs. He saw the chair tipped over in the middle of the floor. He saw the blood spatter, the discarded duct tape, the syringe that had been broken underfoot at some point.

But no Danny.

"Vince?"

He turned. One of the SWAT team guys was holding up a phone. The phone was live with a call.

"It's not good news," he said.

IN THE hills above the canyons, built to feed into the Los Angeles storm drain system, there stand the debris basins. Dry craters of earth and concrete dug there to protect the houses below. When flash floods follow wildfires they get filled up with mud, boulders, and the occasional automobile from the mountain slopes. Occasionally they need to be cleared. A body washed down or dumped there might eventually be bulldozed up and its component parts scattered back into the wild.

Unless it's discovered first.

The drive up the foothills road was a short one. Vince saw the chain link gates standing open and the clearance crew by their trucks, waiting for instructions. He left his car and walked up to the basin's edge, didn't pause there but started on down toward the coroner's yellow tent. A woman in a one-piece scene suit climbed up to meet him and started to explain something, but fell silent and hung back when she picked up on his mood. Vince made it the rest of the way alone, skidding and stumbling down to where the body lay.

THE NEXT THING YOU SEE WHEN YOU DIE

Here was the low point by the drain channel where random garbage gathered, pebbles and twigs and litter and plastic bottles, as undignified a resting place as it was possible to imagine. The body was face-down and badly contorted. When found it had been covered over with a couple of tree branches but someone—the clearance crew or maybe the coroner's people—had moved those aside.

Vince dropped to a crouch alongside and hung his head.

From somewhere upslope, the indistinct sound of a car radio call.

"May God forgive me, Danny boy," Vince said. "I am so sorry."

He knew it was wrong by all the rules but he reached out and placed a hand on the young man's shoulder. Gripped it in a final touch, a last farewell.

And in what he could see of Danny's battered and dirt-encrusted face, a living eye cracked open.

2

SHE WAS DARK and trim and wore a pressed white coat over scrubs with a name tag that he couldn't read from here. Danny hadn't seen her before. The two cops on the door were giving her the full ID check and getting radio clearance before they'd let her into the room. As he waited, he found the bed control and pressed the button to raise him to a sitting position. He'd been hospitalised for some time now—he'd lost track of how long— and security had been tight from the outset. He wondered if anyone outside of a small circle of doctors and justice even knew he was alive.

He'd had scans and biopsies and they'd kept him on dialysis until his renal function returned. They said his pee was black for a while, though he'd been too far out of it to know. They'd gradually withdrawn pain management until he was left with just a saline drip for the headaches. As soon as he was lucid he began a series of recorded depositions for a rotating team of federal prosecutors. No one said as much, but he reckoned they wanted backup testimony in case he didn't make it. The faces changed but the one constant was Sergeant Vince Taylor, always there at the back of the room, never interrupting or speaking unless invited.

This new doctor was finally cleared to enter. Now Danny got a proper look at her tag and a waft of her scent as she checked him over; feeling the nodes in his neck, looking into each eye with a scope from her pocket. The name: Simone Ali, MD. The scent: wintergreen, light on his cheek. She'd taken a breath mint knowing she'd be getting in close.

She seemed satisfied with what she was seeing. "You're a lucky man," she said.

"Free cable and a hot doctor," Danny said. "It doesn't get any better."

She let that go by. "I'm not here as your physician, Daniel," she said. "I'm your psychiatrist."

"That's gonna be fun."

"Why do you say that?"

"Daniel's this green young kid I had to put into storage way back when. I barely remember him. Now he has to wake up and live with what the other guy's been doing. A lot of it's not too pretty."

"We can talk about that," she said, and sat back. She took hold of his wrist and checked her watch, taking an old-fashioned pulse. They had machines for that. This felt better.

Danny said, "So is this a psych evaluation?"

"All part of the treatment if you want to stay a cop."

"Given my last six years of education, my other career options are all criminal."

"That doesn't have to be true," she said. "You're young, you're smart. Maybe lose the gang tattoos and you can be anything you want."

"Yeah?" He looked down. His patient gown had a loose V neck and some ink was showing. He'd gone for a pointed dagger crucifix on the front of each shoulder. Nothing like the full back and chest designs sported by Raffi and some of the others, but getting them had clinched his credibility. And the weird thing was that when it came to it, he'd felt no hesitation.

"In a just world you'd come out of this with some kind of an honor," she said. "I think anyone would call you a hero."

"I can think of a few exceptions."

"You need to own it, Danny. What you did, I couldn't do."

"Don't tell me you're soft, I know how doctors train. You cut up dead people."

"You get used to that."

"I couldn't. I freaked over a head in a sack."

"A head? Whose head?"

"They were kidding me. It was only a football. I saw worse things later on."

"We'll get into that," she said. "But don't put yourself down. You were brave enough to volunteer."

"That's not how it went," he said.

"No?"

"The LAPD needed a fluent speaker with a clean history so they lifted me out of training. One of their people came out east to recruit me. I was on a plane that same afternoon. No time for explanations, no goodbyes."

"So now you get to go home. Get on with your life again."

"After all this time I'm sure I'll find a warm welcome."

She picked up on his tone. "Why wouldn't you?"

"Too much has changed. *I've* changed. You know when your neighbor borrows something and doesn't return it and when you finally get it back, it's fucked?"

She waited.

"I'm the thing."

"Oh, Danny," she said, almost as if they were old friends already, and she started making some notes. "Give yourself time to adjust. I've read up on your case. You did good work and upset some bad people."

"I did," he said.

And then, almost blurting it out, "I've seen the dead ones. Should I be telling you that?"

She laid down her notes and gave him her full attention.

"What do you see?"

"The people I betrayed. Is that normal?"

"After what you had pumped into you, probably yes. When you weren't comatose, you were delirious. But you believe what you did was a betrayal?"

"The trust was real. And people died. It's not a question of the rights and wrongs. You form a bond with people that you can't entirely fake. There are moments. You work for their approval. They look out for you, and they mean it. You know it's the job but you still come out feeling like Judas."

"Would you rather be a man with no conscience? What you're describing is only natural. Guilt's a price we pay for having agency in our lives. You need time to get that into its true perspective."

"I'd be happy just to lose the ghosts."

"There are no ghosts, Danny. Just haunted people."

"You know that for a fact?"

"If they were real, they'd be naked. Think about that."

"Wow," he said.

"We'll be talking about this a lot more," she said, "I promise you." And then, "Just the haunted feelings. Don't dwell too much on the naked part."

A couple more checks and then she was done. He asked her to close the door as she left. He could see the shapes of his guards through the frosted glass but they couldn't see back in.

Once she'd gone, he slid her phone out from under the sheets. Right front pocket, three-finger dip, it had been an easy lift. Those six years of criminal life had given him a range of skills beyond those of the average civilian. He rebooted the locked phone into safe mode and opened the browser.

In here they wouldn't allow him a phone of his own. He'd no way of knowing how long he'd have with this one before she noticed it was missing. He entered a name into the search bar. Results started to come up, way too many. To narrow the search he added the name of his home town.

Then the thought—six years. What if she'd married? Changed her name?

But unless it had happened in the last couple of months, she hadn't.

There she was, name still the same, looking not much different, tagged in someone's Facebook photo. Her own account had privacy set up but on LinkedIn he found the bare bones of a career path with a current workplace listed. He had no way of being sure it was up to date, but the workplace had a page of its own. A new search brought contact details for it. He hesitated at this point.

But not for long. One more touch and he was making the call.

Someone picked up and he heard, "*City Attorney's office, Bob Lambert speaking.*"

Danny said, "You have a Beth Franklin working there?"

"*Beth's in a meeting. May I have your name?*"

"No," Danny said, and ended the call.

3

ARMEN HAD BEEN denied bail and they were holding him in the Men's Central Jail, a low-rise concrete wedding cake of a building on Bauchet. He was allowed two visits a week, thirty minutes each, three people max. Rhianna got word that he needed to speak to her. She had to tag along with his first wife and their twelve-year-old on the understanding that they'd give her the last few minutes.

Today she was dressed-up, respectable. She had to get there an hour early and bring a quarter for the security lockers. Nothing came up on her background check and they were ushered through. It was non-contact visitation in a gallery of booths where visitors talked to inmates on a phone, though glass.

The adults argued over child support while Rhianna waited her turn. Armen and his ex-wife had little else to say to each other and the boy scowled at the floor throughout.

When the time came, the two of them left and she slid into place. Armen's prison blues were a size too large. Low on the stool, he might easily have seemed a diminished version of the man she knew. But he had the forearms of a stevedore and a brow set for thunder. The riveted strength of the cage only made the beast inside it seem more powerful.

"Rhianna."

"Armen."

"I'm sorry you had to sit through that."

"It's not my business. I didn't even listen."

He said, "I wanted you to hear this from me. My lawyers say it's possible the cop didn't die in that *accident*." He made a one-handed air quote with the hand not holding the phone.

"Excuse me?"

"Danny Undercover. They don't know it for sure but we're seeing evidence they could only be getting from him."

This wasn't what she'd been expecting. She took a moment to absorb it.

She said, "How could that happen?"

"I don't know, but if it's true he's a problem. I can't say any more than that." In here it was best to assume that their conversation might be monitored. He went on, "But I thought you deserved to know. Given everything that happened with Nico."

She nodded, slowly, still processing.

Then she said, "It's good if he's alive."

Now it was Armen's turn to be surprised. "Why?"

"I thought him dying would fix it for me. But it hasn't."

Armen studied her through the glass. He seemed to glimpse the terrible bleakness inside her. "So?"

"I need more," she said.

THE NEXT THING YOU SEE WHEN YOU DIE

"That may be," he said. "Right now we have a problem. We need to know for sure if he's still around. If he is, they've got their witness. Miami and Denver have their own problems, but he's ours. And we can't get to—" He caught himself, and chose his words with more care. "We can't reach out to him if no one knows where he is."

A guard passed behind Armen, slowly patrolling the rows of inmates. The prisoner gallery faced out both ways. Beyond the guard was another line of blue-shirted backs, all hunched over their phones and facing glass.

She said, "You want me to find him? Is that why I'm here?"

Armen held her gaze, speaking slowly and deliberately. "No, Rhianna," he said. "I would never ask you to do such a thing." But he was nodding just slightly as he said it.

With just a couple of minutes of the half-hour left they discussed other matters. A message to get to Armen's brother. Papers for the lease on his Lexus. And when the time was up she said, "Why me?"

"You're one motivated soul, Rhianna," he said.

And an expendable one, she thought. But that was okay.

"Got it, chief," Rhianna said.

VINCE CAME to visit, bringing paperwork. Danny was feeling stronger now and had begun some physical therapy starting in the closed-off pool, just him and his guards like some billionaire recluse. He understood that his situation was tricky, politically. He was the youngest of the handful of recruits with the language and cultural background for the job. They'd taken him out of training and then covered his tracks and banked his pay while they hit the Pause button on his life. Now there was all this stuff he needed to read and sign, just to catch up.

While Vince was looking through the sheaf of papers Danny hooked the neck of his gown and was looking down inside it, wondering how the crucifix tattoos would play in his life from here on. Most of the time they'd go unseen. But they'd be part of him, still.

"What do you think?" he said. "Keep 'em or lose 'em?"

Vince looked up. "I do hope we're talking about the ink."

Danny let the shirt fall back. "I just want it to be over," he said.

"Once you testify, it will be."

"They say it'll take the best part of a year to put the case together." Danny glanced toward the door. The original police guard had now been replaced by private security, an odd bunch. Some of them might talk to him, others wouldn't. He didn't rate their chances if any of his old gang showed up. He said, "I can't take a year of this."

"Here's the plan," Vince said. "Soon as the quacks give you the all-clear you'll go back East, rejoin your old department. They'll give out a cover story for your absence."

"Does Armen know I'm alive?"

"Rules of Disclosure mean his defense will have to be told but not your real name or where you're from. Trust me, Danny. You'll be three thousand miles away and back among your own."

"That'll be something. A regular cop's all I ever wanted to be."

"A regular cop has to go through regular training. Yours got cut short. But they'll find something for you to do."

Danny tilted his head back, looking for his future in the off-white of the ceiling. "It's gonna take some getting used to."

"They've given you a shrink?"

"Everything they think I need."

"Call me anytime you need to talk," Vince said. "And you will."

When Vince left him, Danny turned on the TV and then didn't look at it. In the afternoon he was due another therapy session, and after that he'd be allowed a walk. This was worse than jail. He'd envisioned his recovery as some kind of a hero montage, crushing weakness with hard exercise in the confines of his room. He'd tried pushups and collapsed, trembling, on the second. Since then he'd persisted, and now he could manage three.

Everything they think I need.

In their sessions Simone Ali quizzed him about his dreams, and he told her as much as he wanted her to hear. But they were more than dreams. No dream was so intense. Figures with faces, sometimes without. The dead who wouldn't leave. Swarming in his mind, rifling through his memories. Scavengers in an empty house, looking for things to hurt him with.

Sometimes he was back there in the bakery room, still beaten, still bound to the chair. As if that frozen moment was his life, and this the delusion.

With an effort he slid from the bed to the floor and tried for pushups. He managed four. Nearly four. That last one surely counted.

4

THE CANYON ROAD was steep in places and her aunt's Hyundai didn't take the corners well. The car was a twelve-year-old sub-compact that might kindly have been described as a beater. After their prison meeting Rhianna had been given the use of it for running Armen's errands and bearing those messages that his lawyers wouldn't touch. Her aunt wasn't happy with the arrangement, but her aunt's husband owed Armen money. So there was that.

The address she sought was up a side lane of mismatched, secret houses, each nested deep in canyon foliage and screened from its near neighbors. The specific property couldn't be seen from the lane but the mailbox was numbered and held shut with a stone. She drove to the dead end at the top of the lane, turned the car around, and parked it behind an RV from where she walked back down to the mailbox. Then up the driveway with its short curve, and the place was revealed.

It was a design from the fifties, wide, low, and Japanese-influenced; neither a palace nor a mansion but in a location that priced it beyond the range of most. The upper story overhung the lower, with a railed wooden balcony that put the basement's windows in the shade. Behind it rose the canyon side, steep and wooded.

The choice wasn't random. Rhianna had picked up a few realty and rentals magazines from a row of free vending boxes outside a fast food place, searching through them to find what she needed. The specific property didn't matter but the canyon location did. She stood with the magazine in her hand, looking around and waiting. There was one vehicle on the apron before the garage, a Range Rover in gold. There was no sound but the sounds of nature, no sense of the canyon road only a short distance away. The house was enclosed in its own pocket world of crickets and heat and deep, dense greenery.

A narrow wrought iron gate was squeezed between the garage block and the main building, through which she could see a rising flight of narrow steps. The gate had a lock. She imagined that all the living and loving must take place up there, the house opening out onto the higher ground around the back.

Perfect.

Rhianna waited, did nothing to call for attention.

Eventually, someone came down.

A short woman with cropped brown hair. Thirty-three, thirty-five maybe. She stayed behind the locked gate and called out, "Can I help you?"

Rhianna turned.

"The realtor said to meet her outside," she said. "I wasn't to disturb the tenants."

"Nobody's called."

"Really? They told me to be here at ten."

The woman was displeased. She said, "Is it about the guest house?" and Rhianna nodded, showing the magazine. "Wait there," the woman said. She moved to go back and then stopped herself. "What name is it?"

"I didn't catch her name."

"I mean yours."

"Celie," Rhianna said. "Celie Turner."

The woman turned and disappeared up the steps, and Rhianna was left to wait a while longer. She watched a hummingbird hover before one of the lower floor windows, perhaps entranced by its own reflection. After a few minutes, the woman came back.

"Well," she said, "they screwed up again. Nobody knows about you."

"Do I need to come back another day?"

The woman stood for a moment or two, weighing Rhianna up. This was the point at which her ruse could come to nothing. She'd dressed to play respectable, but what passed on a prison visit might not cut it here. Then the woman made a decision. She unlocked the gate and came out.

"It's one bedroom, one bath, one occupant."

"Exactly what I'm looking for."

She used the same bunch of keys on an unmarked door to the left of the gate. "This way," she said, pushing it open, and Rhianna followed her in.

In Californian realtor-speak, a guest house for rent covered any self-contained basement, loft, pool house or converted garage that offered accommodation separately from the main residence. In this case, a one-bedroomed apartment under the main building.

Rhianna felt a pang of sickness as they moved through. She'd kill to live in a place like this. Though essentially a basement cut into a hillside, it was light and airy with a generous floor plan. She and Nico had talked about the home they'd have someday but their dreams had been circumscribed, their imaginations bound by the lives they led. Maybe, if Nico had survived, all that might have changed. Their dreams might have grown along with them. This felt like a sideways look into a lost future, and it made her heart ache.

She pushed the feeling down. She didn't need the distraction.

The woman was saying, "A therapist owned the house. She used this part of it to see her patients. She told us a musician had it before her."

"I like the location," Rhianna said. "It's close to my church."

Maybe that was pushing it.

A long lounge with a kitchen nook. A short passageway with a bathroom off it and then, at the end of the building, a spacious corner bedroom with floor to ceiling windows and a private deck just beyond. The bed was unmade, with a bare mattress that appeared to be new. The woman was unlocking the sliding glass doors so they could move outside. "What kind of work do you do?" she was saying.

"I used to work for a family business," Rhianna said as they stepped out. "They had to downsize so I'm striking out on my own."

THE NEXT THING YOU SEE WHEN YOU DIE

The deck was a modest square with a safety rail and the canyon slope falling away below. A gas barbecue stood in one corner. The feel was almost that of a jungle tree house.

The woman seemed to sense her mood and said, "Nobody overlooks the deck, if that's what's worrying you."

Rhianna looked at the steep canyon wall. Choosing her words with care she said, "I've heard you can get landslides when it rains. Is that ever a problem?"

"Oh, no," the woman said. "We're right below a flood basin. You can't see it from here but it protects this entire neighborhood."

"A flood basin?"

"It doesn't just take rainwater away, it catches any land debris so it never reaches the houses."

"Didn't I hear a story about one of those?" Rhianna said. "They found a body in one. Not too long ago."

"The hiker? That was right up there. Just the other side of those pines."

"I heard it was some criminal gang thing."

"They told us it was a missing hiker. They found him just in time."

"Alive?"

"They airlifted him out. The helicopter came in so low, you could almost touch it going over. They wouldn't risk that for a dead body."

"Wow. Lucky guy. Them finding him in time, I mean."

"You could say that. So…what else I can tell you?"

"I got what I needed," Rhianna said. "Thanks."

RAY'S PARENTS managed an International Deli and Grocery next to a car rental lot on Venice Boulevard. They ran it like a family business, though the actual owners lived in Florida. Like many of the small fry Ray had been granted bail, with conditions. A little luck and a lot of caution had kept Rhianna from being scooped up with the rest of them. She never left prints, or gave a good angle to any camera. And if anyone tried to offer a description of her…well, she had one of those faces.

She could see Ray hauling out trash for curbside collection as she approached the store. Those skinny jeans fit awkwardly over his ankle bracelet. Court-appointed electronic monitoring was one of his bail conditions. Move too far from a designated location and it would broadcast an alert.

"Hello Ray," she said, startling him.

"Rhianna," he said, and then quickly checked all around. "You don't want to be seen here."

"Don't worry about me," she said.

"I'm not," he said, "I'm worried about me."

"I'll keep it brief," she said, and at that moment a voice came from within the store, *Ray? Who are you talking to?*

"It's a friend, Momma," Ray called out, and then with low urgency to Rhianna: "What do you want?"

"The phone that got Nico killed," she said. "Who has it now?"

"Don't ask me. I don't know."

"Can you find out?"

"Why?"

THE NEXT THING YOU SEE WHEN YOU DIE

"Danny Undercover didn't come from nowhere. Six years living a lie, there had to be at least one time when he'd need to call home. There's like three public payphones left in the whole of California. So I'd say that burner is the one he'd use. Who's got it?"

"Leave it be, Rhianna, I've got troubles enough. I'm not looking for more."

She grabbed him by the front of his shirt and before he knew it, they were walking. He stumbled along with her until he could pull away in a panic.

"Hey!" he said. "I go past a hundred feet, they strike out my bond!"

"Armen's lawyer thinks the cop didn't die. I checked and it's true. He didn't."

"I heard about it, they screwed up. We're all sorry."

"Not me. I'm glad he's alive."

"Why?"

"I thought killing him would be the answer. But it wasn't. Now I've got a second chance if I can find him. Leela's cousin says they had a Patient X behind a lot of security at Cedars-Sinai, but he's been discharged now. So where's the cop's phone?"

"Don't do this."

"You want to see him come back and testify?"

"You don't care about that. You just want your revenge. You're gonna make it worse for everyone."

She stepped close and looked into his eyes. She took his hand and he thought she was about to clutch it to her heart and speak, then realised too late that she'd caught his thumb in what now became a painful hold. He squawked and protested as she pulled him further along the sidewalk until he panicked and managed to shake her off, already past the Brazilian café next door and at the limit of his invisible tether.

"All right!" he said, nursing his hand and backing up into safety. "Nico asked the guys in the bakery to crack the passcode."

"Who's got it now?"

"I don't know. One of them. Seriously, I don't know."

I can do this, Nico, she thought. *Not for them, but for you. They want me to kill him, but I can do better. I'll do to him what he did to me.*

Find the thing that he loves, and destroy it.

"Make me a list," she said.

5

HIS FLIGHT WAS delayed so he missed his Atlanta connection and spent four hours waiting for the next plane out, dozing in empty seating by an empty gate. He'd no luggage to speak of, just a sports bag of spare clothing and basic essentials, but that's how it goes, he thought, when you walk out of a story. They'd given him new ID and a prepaid credit card to keep him afloat until his bank details were straightened out, which meant that he'd been able to pick up something to eat. With his six years' worth of unclaimed salary he'd have no money worries for a while. There had been a stash of hard currency hidden away in his room over the hardware store, all of it the product of criminal enterprise, but that had gone in the raids.

The bus that covered the final leg of his journey got in just after midnight. His home town had once boasted an elegant brick bus station, but that building was now a jewelry store and the present terminal was just a gas station with a pickup point. At this hour the shutters were down on the Eagle Mart and there was almost no one around, just an old man waiting by the ice machine.

They'd never been a family of huggers. But at this late hour, and for this one occasion, Danny and Joe Kasabian made an exception.

"Good to have you back," Joe said. "Let's go home."

They walked to the car. Danny said, "Do I get my old room?"

"Still there and waiting for you to pick up your underwear. No one else would volunteer."

His dad still had the old Buick. At the time of Danny's recruitment his mother had been alive, though already ill. That was when Danny had mistakenly thought the job might be all over in a few weeks, months at the most. Vince had fixed it for him to come home for the funeral, but that had literally been a one-day thing. His father had always known the score with his undercover work. But that didn't make it any less hard.

THAT NIGHT Danny slept in his old bed, and in the morning he woke late. For a while he just lay there, taking it in. The shape of the room and the feel of the sheets. The white noise of the suburb beyond his window, all yard sounds and birdsong. He got up, drew the blinds, looked out, and saw clouds.

Joe had waited for a while and then gone ahead with coffee and toast rather than disturb his sleeping son. There was a place set for Danny on the breakfast bar with enough baked goods, cereal and fruit to feed a family for a day. Then Joe produced some bacon, and with a rattle of claws on the hard floor Danny found he had the new family member's full attention. Rufus was a rescue, a retriever-husky mix with ice-blue eyes in a big-boned frame.

Danny put together a bacon sandwich, his every move watched with laser-like intensity. He said, "All those years you wouldn't let me have a dog."

"He's my lifesaver," Joe said. "I took him in after your mother passed."

That hit a raw spot. Danny's mother had never been in the best of health, but her decline had been unforeseen and rapid. Joe, in denial right up to the end, had left Danny out there in the dark until it was too late. Simone Ali had pressed him to talk about it. In the process he'd begun to understand how he'd felt detached from the tragedy, his ability to mourn somehow compromised. Even now it felt like Joe's loss first and foremost, and only then his own.

He said, "I wish I could have kept her in the picture." And then to avoid saying more he reached to scratch the dog's head. Rufus ducked and dodged his hand. "Your dog hates me," he said.

"He likes everybody," Joe said. "He just loves bacon more. What happens now?"

A good question. "I'm still a cop," Danny said.

"After what you've done for them, they should make you a detective."

"Mine's not that kind of experience, Dad. I've never punched a clock or worn a uniform. This is gonna be interesting."

"Just 'cause you're the new boy, don't let them push you around."

"As if. Can I get a ride into town?"

"You can, but Rufus likes to sit in front."

"I'm sure Rufus can learn his place."

THE DOG was first in and there was no moving him. Danny gave up and rode in the back. He'd have to check out car dealerships as soon as his money came through. Rufus sat upright throughout the ride. When the Buick took a bend he'd quietly extend a paw and brace himself against Joe's thigh.

Joe dropped Danny off outside a low square building on a pleasant street lined with greenery. Its official title was the Public Safety Administration Building but everyone called it the Hall of Justice. Along with the town's police headquarters it housed a small jail, two courtrooms, the county attorney's office, and the probation service. There was also traffic enforcement and a dropbox for FBI mail to be forwarded to the regional office in Charlotte.

The police department had a roster of fifty officers plus civilian employees. Had Danny ever completed his training, he might have been given his first assignment here. Suppose he'd stayed. Worn the uniform, worked through his probation, taken his place in the community. What would his life be like now?

As ever, he quickly moved to shut down the thought.

He'd wondered about this moment. While he wouldn't say he felt nervous, he didn't feel comfortable either. The clerk ran off a temporary building pass, and while he waited for a civilian staffer to arrive and take him to his captain's office he saw several people coming and going. They greeted the desk clerk with easy familiarity and to Danny they paid no heed at all.

He studied the board. Under the various headings he saw a sub-heading of *City Attorney's Office* with the location *Rooms 235–239*.

THE NEXT THING YOU SEE WHEN YOU DIE

Then the clerk arrived for him, and they went on up.

Captain Carol Connor was a woman in her forties who wore her brown hair short and her lipstick red. She had an open folder on the desk before her, and looking it over she said, "What we've got here is your cover story. If anyone asks, you've spent the last three years as a safety agent with the State Police Fugitive Unit. If they try calling Harrisburg to check up on you there's a whole made-up history on file. Anything further back, call it training."

Danny said, "What's a safety agent?"

"Nobody knows, so no one can pin you down. It's vague enough to pass and it'll kill anyone's interest. I don't exactly look at you and think safety, but what do I know. Just go with it." She closed the folder and pushed it across to him. "Read and remember," she said. "As far as anyone else is concerned, that's your life so far."

"Okay," he said.

She paused for a moment.

Then she said, "Here's my problem. When the LAPD took you for undercover they bumped you up a grade despite the fact that you never took any of the tests. So I've got to fit you in but I'm not sure how. Why'd they reach out so far to get you, anyway?"

"Language skills, mainly," Danny said. "My grandparents came over to join us and they barely spoke any English. They looked after me while my parents worked. I was at the age where you just pick it up."

Captain Connor swung her chair around and rose to her feet. She opened her door and called out, "Detective Lee? When you've a moment."

She left the door open and returned to her chair. "Belinda Lee will be your supervisor. She knows as much as she needs to, and enough not to ask questions."

This was beginning to feel less like a homecoming, more like the creation of a new cover.

Detective Belinda Lee appeared in the doorway. A square-set Chinese American woman in her thirties, she looked Danny over and said, "Is this the boy?"

"Try not to break him," Captain Connor said.

Belinda Lee motioned for him to follow. He gathered his folder and moved to catch up. The office was bright, laid out in an open plan. As they crossed the floor Detective Lee said, "Detectives Beaman. Ericsson."

Both men were on their phones. Both waved. Both were clean-cut Sunday-best detectives, the kind he'd often seen on *48 Hours*.

She led him out of the office and along the corridor to an unmarked door. She opened it and they entered a poky room all in shadow. As she went to raise the blind she said, "They told me to keep you out of sight until your cases come to trial."

"That could take years," Danny said. "I didn't come home to hide."

The light from the window revealed a desk, a chair, boxes of copying paper piled high, and a dusty Christmas tree. On the table a lamp, textbooks, a legal pad, and a pencil.

Detective Lee said, "We'll get you a computer in here," and she indicated the books. "Those are your manuals. There's seven hundred and fifty hours of training to catch up on. For each test you need to score seventy-five percent or higher."

"Seriously?"

"Read me my rights."

Danny was about to speak, but then hesitated.

She said, "You hear it every day on TV. Five times a night if it's CBS. Believe me, I get that you bring your field experience, but you're going to struggle doing any kind of police work without the background. We live by procedure, here, or we get our cases thrown out of court. Are you carrying?"

Without waiting for an answer she stepped in and checked him for a concealed weapon. He was caught off-guard as she pulled a compact pistol from the small of his back.

"Really?" she said.

"I've been places," he said. "It got to be a habit."

"To carry a weapon on duty you need to qualify," she said. "The range is in the basement. The armourer's a retiree, he just works a couple of mornings a week so you need to catch him. Welcome home."

HE SAT behind the desk and opened the folder to read his new history. Safety agent. It could mean anything from spy to school crossing guard. The captain was right, anyone quizzing him socially was guaranteed to change the subject in a minute or less. Then he went through the drawers. Nothing in the first but yellowing papers and a broken stapler. While poking around in the second he used his free hand to call Vince Taylor.

"Hey," Vince said. "First day. How's it going?"

Danny said, "My dad's replaced me with a dog, and now my supervisor took my gun. The dog has more dignity."

"How are you sleeping now?"

"Still not great. Tell me it gets better."

"It can take a while."

"So how's retirement?"

"Water's high and dirty," Vince said. "No point in going out when the fish can't see the fly."

"Did you buy that boat? You should get a cabin. One of those cabins in the swamp. They've got a name, don't they? What do they call them?"

"You call that a camp."

"I'm picturing you with a deck and a barbecue and tonight you'll watch the sunset. I'm dying with envy."

"Try not to die. I can't take it a second time. Call me whenever you need to talk, Danny. Call me anyway."

"Listen," Danny said. "I've never said this. I appreciate how you hung in for me. I know you could have retired a long time ago."

"What else could I do? My nightmare scenario was some ambitionist taking you over to beef up his resume. You were always gonna need someone who'd been through it himself."

They talked for a while longer with little to say and then they wound up the call. Former Sergeant Vince Taylor was still there in his North Hollywood apartment and they both knew it. He'd always talked about the boat, the lazy days to come. But it was one thing to dream about being aimless, another to face it. Much as Danny had been his mission, he'd also been Vince's excuse.

Ambitionist? Was that even a word?

Someone from technical services showed up an hour later with a well-used monitor and keyboard and a selection of cables. By then Danny was grateful for the sight of another human face. He tried some small talk but the computer guy's conversation was limited to stupid mistakes with computers and the people who made them. Danny left him to work and wandered back down the corridor to the main office. The only person there now was Belinda Lee, and she was talking on her phone.

"Yeah," she was saying. "Have they set a date for that?"

She frowned up at Danny as he appeared before her. He leaned over to scan her desk. Policing still created a lot of paperwork, but Detective Lee was well organised. Danny located her *In* tray and made a show of delicately lifting the corner of the top item to see the next.

Without interrupting her call, Belinda Lee leaned forward and swatted his hand away.

Danny remained unfazed. With the phone still at her ear, Belinda Lee made a silent *What?* face.

Danny pointed to her case files and then to himself. His message was clear. *Give me something to do.*

To her caller she was saying, "It's just a day to them, but you add in the travel and that's three days out of my week. They need to clear it with my boss." And as she was speaking she was reaching forward and pulling out a thin file from under the others. She handed it to Danny and signalled for him to go. Anything to end the distraction. Anything to get rid of him.

He didn't leave, not right away. He opened the folder and glanced down the first page. A dead homeless man. He looked up from the page and she waved him away, her message clear. Did he think she'd trust him with anything more? It was the best he was going to get.

Danny mimed a steering wheel.

Her car keys were lying on her desk. She grabbed them away before he could get any further ideas.

On his way out of the office he noted an unattended fob on another desk. He scooped it up in passing.

6

DANNY STOOD ON the spot where the dead man had been found, and looked around. There was fast traffic roaring by overhead, and slow traffic at nearby lights where this road passed beneath the freeway. The scrub patch had been cordoned off with crime scene tape. The tape was days old, ripped and broken. Beyond that he'd found nothing.

This had been one man's last sight of his world. A homeless man, which for many erased any sense of identity or importance. But the word was just a label on a long human story, often as rich as it was tragic. The body had lain undiscovered for some time within a few yards of the road, mostly concealed by low scrub. The notes told of a man of around fifty, shabbily dressed and unkempt to a degree that indicated neglect. He'd taken a beating and probably lay injured for hours before expiring. Neither his prints nor his DNA were on file and he'd had no useful dental work.

Down at the stoplight there was a thin black man in a wool cap working the line, moving down the middle from car to car with a paper cup as the traffic waited out the light. It was hard to see from here who was giving, and who was turning away. They were all getting the same *God bless you.*

Danny had passed an old-style diner on the way here. Ten minutes later he was back, crossing the scrub with a coffee cup in each hand. Traffic was moving and the Thin Guy had retreated from the road to a spot under the freeway where he'd set a folding chair rescued from trash. He was counting his change, but he stopped to watch as Danny approached.

"It's not a shakedown," Danny called out. "I'm a cop."

The Thin Guy called back, "You say it like the two things are mutually exclusive."

Danny reached him and handed over one of the coffees. The Thin Guy nodded his thanks, but he remained suspicious. He wasn't young, but nor was he as old as his movements had made him seem.

Danny said, "You know about the dead man they found over there? Did anybody speak to you about him?"

"I saw when they took him away."

"Did you know him?"

"He and I may have had some words in the past. Nothin worth takin a person's life for."

"What were those words about?"

"Workin my cars, tryin to sell a wristwatch. Which he probably stole. That was a week ago and we did not argue. He went away when I asked him to."

"What was he like?"

"Well spoken. Wouldn't look you in the eye."

"You know his name?"

THE NEXT THING YOU SEE WHEN YOU DIE

A shake of the head. "You should check out the hobo camp on Technology Drive. I think he was one of those homeless people." He saw Danny's look and said, "I'm not homeless. I live with my daughter. I just can't get work."

The hobo squat was a schoolbus junkyard in an area of derelict factories. With canvas and salvaged furniture the buses had been turned into shanty homes. It was a relatively recent development, sprung up in the time that Danny had been away, and some dozens of people had found a place here. Danny got into a conversation with a Grapes-of-Wrath family in the company of a priest wearing a zippered fleece over his clerical collar.

The woman of the family said, "I don't mean to be unhelpful, but how can we tell you we saw a person if you don't have a picture?"

"The picture wouldn't be much help," Danny said. "His face was too messed up."

"You can fix all that and photoshop the eyes open," a younger man suggested.

Danny said, "This man had a wristwatch he was trying to sell. Do you know anything about that?"

"We don't countenance thieves around here," the woman said.

"I don't believe he stole it," Danny began, but before he could press it any further he heard, *Danny? Danny Kasabian?*

He turned.

And there she was.

ACROSS THE open space behind him, Beth Franklin. The one and only. Dressed down and bundled up against the weather but unmistakably Beth.

She was standing in a gap between buses where some old chairs had been set up around a burned-out campfire. Alongside her stood a wiry young man with a cast on his arm. She'd been showing him some printed literature. Some kind of church stuff or legal advice, from the looks of it. Unless she'd found Jesus in the past half dozen years, legal advice was the more likely.

She was staring, almost uncomprehending.

Danny raised a hesitant hand.

With a sudden shift in her priorities, she dumped the printed matter onto the wiry young man and told him, "Read the forms. I'll get back to you."

And now she was coming over. Danny moved away from the family he'd been talking to, drawing Beth aside to meet him on neutral ground.

She was shaking her head in angry disbelief.

"Hello, Beth," he said, braced for impact.

"'Hello Beth'?" she said. "Are you for real?"

"Give me a chance to explain?"

"Explain? You know what? It's history now. I don't need to hear it. Just like I heard no warning, no apology, not even a goodbye."

"I wanted to call."

"So why didn't you?"

"It could have been risky for both of us. What were you told?"

"That they'd moved you off to do some training somewhere. I was supposed to believe you weren't allowed your phone."

"That part's true, for security. They actually took it away in case I got tempted."

"Don't bullshit me, Danny. You disappear one night and show up five years later."

"It's six."

"Six years! What am I supposed to think?"

"I know it's too late to say it, but I'm sorry."

"You're right. It's too late. You break up with a person face to face. You don't run off and hide until they give up and dump you. Even your dad couldn't tell me anything. I showed up on your parents' doorstep like some fucking waif. I can't believe I did that."

"Believe this or don't, Beth. What happened to us was not my choice. I got played the duty card and from then on my life wasn't my own. I never knew what they told you and I thought it would be something I could fix. They promised me I'd be home before the end of the year."

"And why now?"

"It's finally over. Kind of. More or less."

"You don't get to just walk back in. You'd better not be thinking that."

"Trust me, I'm not. Can we at least talk?"

"About what?"

"Oh, come on. You have questions. And I owe you answers."

Someone was trying to get her attention. She had more to do here. But she agreed to meet him at the diner.

1

IT WAS THE same diner, the one where he'd picked up the coffee. It was nothing fancy. She met him outside and they went in and took a booth. By now she'd simmered down somewhat. Danny had been advised not to share the truth about his absence with anyone beyond immediate family. He was choosing to ignore the advice. After what he'd put her through, Beth deserved nothing less.

He warned her to keep his story to herself. Spreading it around could give him real problems. She said okay and waited, stone-faced, to hear his excuses. So then Danny explained something of the operation he'd been involved in, telling her of his recruitment, of the life he'd led as a Level 1 UC, and of the headline-grabbing nationwide sweep that had brought it all to an end.

He could see the wheels working as she listened. Gang crime? Undercover work? It was a lot to take in with only his word to go on. She wasn't one of those women who could be talked into believing that secret agent work explained their loser boyfriends.

There came a point where he felt he'd said enough. He chose to skip the part about his unmasking and final ordeal.

"It was a major operation," he said. "You honestly never heard of it?"

"LA news doesn't make the front pages here."

"It wasn't just LA."

Even if he made her believe him it was a big ask, inviting her to reframe her private pain in such a broad context. So it was no surprise when she brought it back to the immediate and personal, saying, "I couldn't believe you'd do that to me. No warning, no apology, not even a goodbye."

"I wanted to call," Danny said. "But my handler said it's the classic way for a cover to get blown."

"Your handler."

"You think I'm making this up."

She had to take a moment. He waited. She'd had six years to imagine all kinds of scenarios, and he doubted that any of them would have been close to what she'd just heard.

She said, "You really hurt me, Danny. What did you expect me to think?"

"The more it went on, the deeper in I got," he said. "There comes a point where you feel you've missed the chance to put things right."

"Not even a message?"

"You really think I didn't want to? When I finally got the opportunity I called your office from the hospital. Some guy put me off."

"That would be Bob," she said, and then belatedly, "The hospital?"

"It didn't end well."

He shrugged off the chance to go into detail, but she'd picked up something of the darkness that lay behind this. She was looking at him differently now. For a moment he avoided her eyes.

She said, "I guess it was no picnic for you either."

"It wasn't fun. If that's any compensation."

"That's not fair. You know me better than that."

"Yeah. Sorry."

"Look, I have to be somewhere." She turned to her shoulder bag and rummaged around amongst the leaflets and brochures, finally coming out with a printed card. She held it out and said, "Don't read to much into this. There may be times when we have to work together. So take my number in case you need to call again."

Danny took the card and read the print. "Victim support?" He wasn't sure what to make of that.

"It's my job now," she said. "That's my direct number. I follow up with the injured party after a crime. Arrange for counselling. Help them make a claim. Whatever they need. It's useful work."

His gaze had strayed past the card to the hand that gave it. No wedding band. Without realising it, he kept looking for long enough to give himself away.

Beth said, "I do have a partner. His name is Rick. He's a paramedic."

Danny nodded. Yeah, fine, right. "Any kids?"

"No."

"But he's the one."

"Yes," she said firmly. "He's the one."

"All worked out for the best, then."

"In the end."

"I'm happy for you," he said. Then, "Seriously, he sounds great. I was never going to be a good bet. You're way better off."

"Don't put yourself down."

"You know me. It's what I do."

There seemed to be nothing more that either of them could say. "Well…" She was getting ready to leave. "I'll see you, Danny."

"Yeah."

He stayed for a while. Watched her go, through the window.

So she'd been to his dad. His father hadn't mentioned that. Joe had been briefed on what to say. He would have told her that his son had been called to work away, and no more. But she was bright, always had been brighter than Danny, and he wished that maybe at some level she might have worked it out for herself. She'd pleaded ignorance but, seriously, the raids had been all over the news.

All of which meant nothing if she really had moved on.

He'd once spoken to Vince of his fears of getting in too deep, of losing sight of the way back. During his time under cover he'd sustained himself with thoughts of his return. The lower the moment, the more sentimental the fantasy. Always with Beth. He was home, she'd been waiting. Or he was hurt, and she found him. In facing her now he'd opened the Schrödinger box, and all those imagined worlds of possibility had collapsed down into this one hard reality.

THE NEXT THING YOU SEE WHEN YOU DIE

She'd almost certainly go online, looking to verify what he'd told her. Well, good. But picking up his life where he'd left off—that had never been a realistic option. He had to accept that now. He felt like a wedding guest showing up to an empty tent to find the tables all cleared and his gift unopened.

Initial burst of anger apart, she'd been pretty adult about the whole thing.

He picked up the check and went to the counter to pay. He ought to head back, along the way maybe put in some gas to mollify the vehicle's owner, but he needed some time to process.

He was going to miss her. They'd been as close as any two young people could be. Each of them the other's first lover, the sharer of their dreams, their confidante. Things he could tell no one else, he'd told to Beth. Now he didn't even have Vince for that, and he wasn't about to worry his dad. And as for his therapist back in LA—Simone was a good person and she meant well, but forget it. For her it was a job. He'd just have to carry the bad stuff with him, holding it close until it faded, or sank back in.

He sat in the car in the diner's parking lot. The bad stuff. When they'd left him alone in that back room of the bakery, taped to a chair with toxic fire surging through his veins, they'd imagined him unconscious. He wasn't, but nor was he entirely present. It was as if he was detached from his body, aware of it, occupying the same space, but no longer firmly anchored. The pain had begun the process of driving him out of its shell. He realised that he was dying.

With that knowledge he raised his head and saw them. He could picture them now. Those mute figures, standing before him.

Anita the closest, leaning forward to stare into his eyes with a bereaved mother's fury. Armen had said they'd be waiting for him, and here they were.

They were patient. Looking for him to get his dying done, so they could have him.

He started the car. Maybe he'd just drive around for a while. Maybe track down the remains of his homeless victim.

Then there was that one night in the hospital. It seemed that some lapse on the part of the private security team had left him unguarded and unattended in the small hours. By then his strength had begun to return and he was getting antsy. He saw an opportunity to get out of the room and go for an unsupervised wander, and he took it. Just a little taste of freedom was all he craved. Not that he had the energy for much more.

All the lights were on in the corridor outside, but it was empty. The tile was cold under his bare feet. As he moved along he stayed within reach of the wall, just in case. Signage with wayfinder arrows at the corridor's end pointed him toward the cafeteria.

Which was also silent at this hour. The counters had been cleaned down. There was a row of snack vending machines but he had no money. At the end of the row stood an ATM but he had no card. Behind the glass of the first machine he could see coconut water, kombucha, San Pellegrino, Larabars. So very California.

He had that sense of being watched and when he turned to look, there they were. Seated at the empty tables, staring at him. Each alone apart from Pete Krikorian, who had Beth beside him.

THE NEXT THING YOU SEE WHEN YOU DIE

It was Beth from before, the nineteen-year-old of memory, not the woman he'd met tonight. She was the only one of them not looking directly at him. Danny was aware of speaking her name, although he seemed to make no sound. Beth started to rise but Pete quietly placed his hand on her shoulder, and she sank back to her seat.

Danny didn't remember returning to his room. Of course it had to be some kind of a nightmare driven by medication and trauma, but the night security team was fired and replaced the next day and even Vince couldn't tell him why.

He should maybe stay away from her now.

She'd moved on.

So it shouldn't be that hard.

8

THE HOMELESS VICTIM had been removed to the County Medical Examiner's facility for autopsy and storage. While a John or Jane Doe case would stay open indefinitely, the actual remains would be kept for only a month and then, if unclaimed, cremated and the ashes stored along with DNA, hair, and fingerprint samples and photographs of the clothing worn.

Danny had called ahead and there was an assistant waiting to meet him. The mortuary tech unzipped the bag to reveal the body of a middle-aged man, badly beaten and with his general look not improved by the sutured autopsy wound. Taking out his phone to get his own pictures of the victim's face from a few angles, he said, "Are there any personal effects?"

"A cardboard belt and three dollars in change. Is this for online?"

"What?"

"They put the John Does on web sites. So anyone can play detective. This one had money in the past."

"How can you know that?"

The mortuary tech moved around to the end of the table, and with one gloved hand he steadied the cadaver's head while with the other he parted the hair. The resewn scalp was revealed, but that wasn't the point. The hair fell oddly, in neat rows like wheat.

"These hair plugs," he said. "They wouldn't have been cheap, but it's a technique they haven't used in years."

Danny was considering something.

He said, "Can I see his arms?"

"Feel free," the tech said, and waited until Danny's look made it clear that he wasn't about to touch any dead body. So the tech pulled the zip down further and lifted out each arm in turn for Danny's inspection.

Danny leaned in and took the closest look at the left forearm. Then he straightened.

"Okay," he said.

"Seen what you need?"

"I think so."

HE RETURNED Detective Ericsson's car keys with an apology that was as effusive as it was insincere. With everyone present in the office he asked, "Do we keep a list of area pawnbrokers?"

Belinda Lee said drily, "We call that the Yellow Pages."

Danny said, "Your transient man was last seen failing to sell a wristwatch at a road junction. He was not found with a wristwatch."

"You're thinking he pawned it?"

"It's possible that the person who took it from him may have tried to."

Detective Lee reached down into a drawer and brought out an honest-to-God actual phone book, some years old and looking unused. She dropped it on the desk and said, "Knock yourself out."

A phone book? Really? Okay. He took it up and started to skip through the pages, looking for the relevant section and saying, "He'd had a better life once. The wristwatch could have been his last connection to it."

"If it was his own."

"There was a tan line on his left arm," Danny said. "He'd been wearing it."

He was still leafing through the book when Detective Beaman called across the office and said, "Every pawnbroker and jewelry dealer in the area makes a weekly police report. Has to be in by 10 a.m. Tuesday." He looked at Belinda Lee. "You weren't going to tell him?"

Belinda Lee shrugged.

Danny tossed the book.

"Thanks," he said, and was gone.

The computer tech had completed his work. The terminal in his glorified store cupboard down the corridor was up and running, and he was able to call up the latest set of dealer reports. Nothing about a wristwatch on offer, suspicious or otherwise. He posted a notice to be flagged with any new information.

And there it was. Danny's first big case, and he'd gone about as far as he could with it. This shouldn't have felt personal, but somehow it did.

After all, there wasn't much to choose between lying dead in a highway no-man's-land and being left for dead in a public drain.

It was not lost on him that this man's fate—beaten, abandoned, forgotten—might so easily have been his own.

9

BETH TOLD RICK, "I went straight back to the office and threw up. I wasn't expecting that."

"You threw up in the office?"

"Not in the actual office. I made it to the toilet first. Jesus. Imagine living *that* down."

They were in their apartment that evening. Dinner was cleared and the TV was on and they were sitting on the couch, not watching it. Beth was unable to concentrate, still dazed after the day's unexpected turn. Rick had his hand on her back, giving her a gentle and affectionate rub that just said, *I'm here.*

Danny's appearance at the homeless camp had shaken her. All of the bad memories of the years before had resurfaced like dead wood in a fetid lake. She'd told him she was now done with him, and she was. But getting there had left its mark.

"Have him over," Rick said.

"Yeah, right."

"I'm serious."

She looked at him. He made a face that said, *Well?*

Rick was four years older, reliable, uncomplicated. They'd met once socially and then again when Janelle had a fainting

69

spell in the office and he was the attending paramedic. Beth had mentioned her place of work in the conversation, and he'd jumped on the call in the hope he might see her there. As they got acquainted he'd noted her pain, he'd taken it slow. Maybe it was the combination of empathy and capability that came along with the job; they were qualities that had gradually come to attract her at a time when she was telling everyone that she'd sworn off men for ever.

She said, "You're not even a little bit jealous?"

"Of the guy you were with since high school? More than a little. I want to see him. I want him to see us."

"I'm over him, Rick. I told him so."

"I know you are."

"You're a good man."

"Not half as good as I look."

They fell silent for a while and let the TV fill the space. She leaned her head against him and he stroked her hair, almost absently. Theirs was a small apartment, just the one bedroom with a tiny bath and kitchen and barely enough space in the hallway for Rick to store his racing bike on the wall. The sitting room was made smaller by the bookshelves they'd bought and the pictures they'd hung to cover the odd stain.

The pictures. One of Beth's showed a grand mansion on the edge of town that had burned down in 1928. A Comfort Inn stood on the spot now. The Franklins had been one of the town's founding families. An ancestor had donated much of the land it was built on, and her great-grandfather had founded the library. But that was all past. By the Second World War the fortune had gone. But all the same, roots go deep.

Rick said, "You ready to turn in?"

"You go on. I'll be along in a while."

He disengaged himself and got to his feet. He lingered in the doorway behind her for a while, sensing a need, uncertain of how to meet it.

She looked back. Gave him a brief smile, to reassure him.

"Go," she said. So he nodded, and went.

She lowered the volume on the TV so it wouldn't disturb him. It was one of the late shows but her attention wasn't on it. The day had shaken her up, more than she wanted to admit. There had been a time when she'd been unable to imagine a life without Danny Kasabian in it. In her high school yearbook, at the place still marked by prom flowers pressed between the pages, a teenaged Beth and Danny were pictured together as "Cutest Couple". And at that time they were, it was true, you couldn't look at the picture and think otherwise.

But seeing Danny today…there'd been a change. It wasn't just the length of his time away that made her think it. He'd grown lean, he seemed edgy. A little scary, even. Whatever his absence had entailed, he'd brought something of it home with him.

Beth was determined not to be haunted by the paths not taken. She'd even told Danny that Rick was the one.

Even though she'd never said as much to Rick.

10

WHEN THE PACKAGE came, Rhianna got to the door ahead of her uncle. She recognised the messenger, a nephew of Armen's with a record as clean as her own. The family had been planning to send him to law school. He said, "They told me to ask for ID." Rhianna said, "Fuck's sake, David," and shut the door in his face.

As she headed back to her room she heard her uncle call out, "Who was it?" and she called back, "Wrong apartment, *Amo*," before she slid in and closed the door. She took her nail scissors from the dresser and sat on the bed to attack the parcel. The outer layer was more brown tape than paper and inside it was a ball of bubble wrap taped just as securely. When she finally reached the heart of the bundle and laid the wrapping aside she was left holding the prize, a Best Buy prepaid thirty-dollar Motorola.

Danny Undercover's burner phone. The one Nico had died for.

There was no charger, no documentation. The techie assigned to crack it had probably wiped everything clean of his own prints, too. Or should, if he had any sense. The phone was basic to the point of being primitive, with the SIM card and battery removed and wrapped separately to forestall any efforts to track it.

On seeing this, she hesitated. Would prosecutors be monitoring the cell networks, waiting for the number to appear online? If she activated it here, the phone might get pinged and draw the authorities to the building. Right to the apartment, even. It seemed a slender chance, but one she wasn't willing to take.

So twenty minutes later she was between two delivery trucks in a parking lot several blocks away, screened from any camera surveillance as she put the handset together. A hooded sweatshirt, and a woollen cap pulled low. She'd make this quick.

The phone powered up and went through its boot routine. There was a good charge on the battery and the techs had done their job, with security taken off and access unlocked. When the screen lit up the call history was all there, deleted contacts and messages restored. She ran down the list of calls. Every one of them to the same anonymous number, a record of all the times that he'd passed on their secrets to those people who controlled him. He'd made his reports every couple of weeks, sometimes more often. She felt the fury of betrayal all over again.

The figures blurred together in vertical lines as she scrolled down, but then a break in the pattern leapt out. She overshot, scrolled back to the one standalone number amongst the regular contacts.

She highlighted the number and hit Call.

After an achingly long wait that was probably only five seconds or less, she got a ring-out tone. She had no idea what might be coming next.

It rang, and kept on ringing.

"Come on, pick up," she breathed. She glanced around. Maybe her caution was edging into paranoia. But if they did zero in her location, with any luck they'd think that the call was made from one of the semis. She'd be long gone and they'd be chasing some hapless trucker all over the county.

Something was happening.

She prepared to speak.

But then a machine cut in and she heard, "*If you've got a message for Joe Kasabian, speak after the tone. If you're calling for Danny, he's got his own damn phone.*"

She cut the call before the beep.

Her heart was racing.

No one had ever expected much from Rhianna. Sometimes she wondered if they valued her at all. No promise of law school for her, it was always the low-level stuff. Card skimming. Loan application fraud. Writing emails for online romance scams with fictitious hotties promising true love for the price of a plane ticket to America. Click on my pics and see what I'm promising, and the pictures were of some more attractive stranger stolen from the web. Since the arrests they'd mostly been using her as a go-between carrying messages from one jail to another.

Yet here she was. And look what she was doing.

Would it be appreciated? She doubted it.

She had all she needed here. Before breaking down the Motorola she took another look at the number to fix it in her memory. It was for a landline with an area code, which was something of a gift. It narrowed her search down from the entire continental USA to one state, maybe a handful of counties.

She put the case of the phone in one pocket, the battery and SIM in the other. Pulled her hood down low and set out from between the trucks to put some distance between herself and this place, just in case. She could look up the area code later.

Joe Kasabian. An older guy, from the voice. The father, most likely.

Which was a good start.

11

THE DAYS PASSED. Outside of work, Danny found it a struggle to settle in. He did make an effort. He met up with a group of his oldest male friends for a pleasant but unsatisfying evening. They now had jobs, wives, children to go home early to. They talked about local sports and people he wasn't familiar with. Danny's best stories were the ones he wasn't allowed to tell. At the approach of eleven they picked over the details of the restaurant bill and parted without any follow-up arrangement beyond a general agreement to do this again. Sometime.

Belinda Lee quickly realised that Danny was pretty much incapable of staying in the office and studying. She sent him out to ride along with Detective Ericsson, who was still sulking over the lifting of his car keys. Their calls were mostly routine, but then there was an interview with the owner of a row house on the fringe of the historic district, where the man was unwilling to endorse the street's concerns about his immediate neighbor. No, he's a good guy, good citizen, if he keeps strange hours that's no business of mine. While Ericsson was asking the questions, Danny was feeling the walls. The party wall was almost hot to the touch. After they'd followed up and busted the unattended cannabis farm next door, the homeowner confessed that he'd ignored the obvious for the sake of the free heat. "This is an old place," he explained miserably. "It costs so much to keep it warm in the winter."

There were a couple of store thefts and one missing pet, mistyped in the report as a missing poet. They were called to a homeowner who'd tired of losing deliveries to porch pirates and had put together a booby trapped parcel and left it out on the stoop. He'd seen YouTube videos of packages rigged with glitter bombs and decided to go one better. But he miscalculated badly and blew off his own front door, plus two of the would-be thief's fingers. The door hung in its frame, the fingers were found in the yard.

Ericsson was nicer to him after Danny gifted him sole credit for the cannabis farm. For his own part Danny didn't care about scoring local points, and was beginning to wonder if there was any future for him in straightforward small-town policing.

He did have his uses. At the start of his third week he was sent to the interrogation suite after a call for a translator. A former priest was suspected of trafficking a young woman who spoke no English. His story was that they'd agreed marriage online after more than a year of corresponding and sharing photographs. He'd signed off on the woman's visa application and sent a ticket for her travel. No one yet knew her side of it, as the agency interpreter from Charlotte hadn't shown up. Danny found the woman alone in the room looking small and scared. By her passport she was just shy of thirty, but across the room she could almost have passed for sixteen.

"It's all right now, sister," he told her. "I'm here to look after you."

His words triggered some measure of relief, and her story came out. She was a single mother with a seven-year-old son who'd paid $5,000 to an online broker on the promise of a green card and employment in the US. The job would involve housekeeping and childcare for an American family. It was a chance to make some money and to learn English while planning a better future. Once settled in, she could send for her boy.

She'd been met at the airport by a man holding a board with her name on it. He'd brought flowers. Her suspicions were raised when they arrived at a house and she saw no sign of any family. The alarm bells went into overdrive when he showed her a cleared half of the closet. Her reading of this was that he expected her to share the bedroom. She ran out into the street and refused to go back in, fearing now for her life. Neighbors called the emergency services.

Danny knew the scam. Armen called it pig butchering, feeding the marks until they walked to their own slaughter. While the "broker" was taking her money, the young woman's photographs and profile were being used to sell her as a bogus bride. Her "green card" was just a tourist visa. Most days she'd have been challenged at the border.

She was scared. She said, "Will they send me to prison?"

"You've done nothing wrong," he said. "I can't promise you'll be able to stay, but I know someone who can help."

He took out Beth's card, wrote his own name and number on the back.

BY NOW the agency translator had appeared. Danny brought her up to speed and went across the hallway to where Samuel Sweeney, formerly Father Sweeney, sat alone in another room. He was around sixty, gaunt, in a black zippered sweater that echoed the clerical garb he'd once worn. He had a paper cup and was drinking water with a shaking hand. He wouldn't meet Danny's gaze. Others might see evasion there; Danny saw shame.

"Walk with me," he said.

"Who are you?"

"Don't worry about that. Just walk with me."

It was two blocks to the nearest bar. The place was all but empty at this hour of the day. As they entered Danny said, "What is it? Whisky?"

Sweeney said, "Can we do this?" and Danny said, "We're doing it."

Danny asked the barman's name and said, "Bring us two glasses and leave the bottle, Renaldo, we've got some business here."

The barman said, "I don't want trouble."

Danny showed his badge and the money. "Trust me," he said.

The barman brought their drinks to a booth and left the bottle, as instructed. Danny pushed both glasses across the table. He watched each shot go down and waited for the effect to kick in.

He said, "Have you ever tried to get sober, Father?"

THE NEXT THING YOU SEE WHEN YOU DIE

"Don't call me that."

"Have you?"

"I was planning to. Given a good enough reason."

"Like a wedding with a woman less than half your age?"

"That's not what this was."

"So set me straight."

Another shot downed, the hand a little steadier.

Sweeney hadn't been looking for romance, just someone to talk to. When you're lonely enough, even a scammer would do. It was a game of pretend between two strangers. Both of them avatars playing their roles, one angling for money, the other finding solace in the conversation. He'd no intention of falling for anything.

Then off-book messages began appearing from a different email account, alerting him to the fraud and warning him not to be taken in. The writer claimed to be one of the women working online for the scam team. She'd felt a connection and didn't want to see him hurt.

He should have known better, should have known where this was going, but good judgment had deserted him long ago. Inevitably those messages were part of a much longer game that had brought him to this point. Her name, her street address, what she mentioned of her history, they all checked out. He fell right into the trap. The end point had been his eventual gift to her, a no-strings marriage of convenience to secure a safer future in America.

"Did you know she has a child?"

"I realise now that I don't know her at all. They were just using her identity."

"You were played, Sam. Both of you played off against each other. You thought you'd found someone to save, she thought she was getting a job and a new life. The first time you had any actual contact was when you mailed her the plane ticket. A smarter criminal would have taken that too."

"This one was smart enough. What will happen to her?"

"I don't know. I've put her in touch with some people. They'll take care of her."

"Can you make sure she understands? I wasn't proposing to share a bed. I had the couch already made up, you can go and see."

"Spoken like a priest."

"I lost my faith long ago," he said, and looked down into the glass. "I filled the void with this. I know it'll kill me and I'm ready to go if I can only do one good thing for someone first. I thought this was my chance but I've blown it."

"Maybe not," Danny said. "See how it plays out from here."

"It's been hard," Sweeney said. "The Church was my family but I was living a lie. You go on as long as you can and then one day you're out. And alone."

"I get it," Danny said.

12

BETH CALLED A meeting with Danny to straighten out details of the young woman's case. She approached it with some slight apprehension. It took place in the conference room of the county attorney's office, just the two of them at one end of a table for twelve.

She made sure to keep it businesslike and formal, sticking to the points. Then at the end of it when they were gathering papers she said, "Rick says I have to invite you over one evening."

"Does he," Danny said. No inflection there. This was only their second encounter and she was finding Danny quite hard to read after his years away.

"He wants to meet you," she said.

"And what do you want?"

Rick was serious about the invitation, and he'd mentioned it more than once. Beth had held out for a while and then she gave in. To keep refusing would be to signal in the wrong way that it mattered.

Which was how, a couple of evenings later, she came to be opening the apartment's door to see Danny standing there with a bottle in each hand.

"I got red, I got white," Danny said. "Don't know what Rick goes for, so I covered all the angles."

"Rick doesn't drink," she said, taking them from him. "But thanks."

Rick was there with a big welcome. She watched them shake hands like a couple of world leaders, Rick with the confidence of the host nation.

At first it seemed to be costing Danny some effort to be sociable, but then she realised that he was probably out of practice. He wasn't used to being himself. Danny of old was a relatively uncomplicated soul. Maybe in time she'd come to understand the cost to him of those years away. For now she'd spent so much of her personal capital dealing with her own pain that there wasn't much left over for his.

It took him half an hour or so to start loosening up. When he told the story of the porch pirate's blown-off fingers, something of the old Danny started to show through.

The food choices were a mix of Indian and Mexican dishes and when Danny gave the usual compliments Beth said, "Well, you know me. I don't cook," and Rick added, "But if Trader Joe freezes it, I can nuke it."

Rick surprised Beth by taking one glass of wine.

Over dinner they talked about movies they each liked, though Danny wasn't entirely up to speed on anything recent. Rick told some of his EMT stories including one about a patient who'd taken LSD and tried to cut off his own arm, believing it was a snake. When he started on his story about the wig and the maggots Beth said, "Change of subject, Rick, we're eating."

THE NEXT THING YOU SEE WHEN YOU DIE

So Danny said, "How did you two meet?"

Rick said, "Beth was falling-down drunk and someone called 911. When I got there she threw up on my uniform."

Beth leaned over and slapped his arm. "Karin Brady introduced us," she said, and to Danny, "You remember Karin?"

Danny said, "The loopy one from law school?"

"My dearest cousin," Rick said, and when Danny tried to backpedal he laughed and Beth said, "No, you're okay. He's telling a lie."

Then Beth was on her feet, giving him a look. "Who wants coffee?" she said, and Rick got the message and started to gather dishes.

They went into the kitchen. She had Rick load the dishwasher while she put grounds in the machine, mainly as a ploy to keep him safely in her sight. One glass of wine. FFS.

"I'm starting to think this was the worst idea," she said, keeping her voice low.

"It's going great for me," Rick said.

"Yeah, I can see that." She threw the switch on the grinder and had to raise her voice just a little. "What do you think? I googled the gang raids he talked about. It all holds up."

"You didn't believe him?"

"Call it due diligence."

"Six years, though," Rick said. "You'd pick up the phone."

"And not one visit home. People say he came back for his mother's funeral. But I don't know anyone who saw him."

When they went back with Rick carrying the tray, Danny had moved to the couch. He was leafing through the pages of the local free newspaper. "Looking for apartments," he explained. "Can't mooch off my dad forever."

Rick said, "Did you see Beth's letter? Page fifteen."

Danny found the page and then said, with surprise, "The library closed?"

"The George W. Franklin Library," Beth said. "The money's all gone but my people damn near built this community. Now developers are wiping out every last trace of what we made. No one else ever speaks out against them. I tried it and what do you think happened? They got a court order on me. Now I can't even go near the building while they tear it to pieces. For a shopping plaza with high-end apartments. They're only keeping the front wall and the expensive marble. The Franklin Library. If you don't count some distant cousins in Canada, I'm the last of the line."

"You know the answer to that," Rick said. "Breed more Franklins."

"You know the answer to *that*," Beth said. "Make more money."

LATER ON, after Danny had said his thanks and goodbyes and how great it was to see the two of them so settled and happy, he went out to meet his Uber and they cleared up and switched off lights. While Rick sat on the bed poking a finger through yet another hole in one of his socks, Beth crawled over in her underwear and put her arms around his neck from behind.

THE NEXT THING YOU SEE WHEN YOU DIE

She said accusingly, "I was drunk and someone called 911??"

"He was *that* close to buying it." He turned around inside her embrace, now to face her. Her sexy underwear was the Macy's three-in-a-pack kind. Real-world sexy once you've added the person inside.

"Hey," she said. "Thanks."

"For what?"

"You know what."

"No big deal. Was he always so…"

"Scary?"

"I wasn't going to say that, but maybe yeah. You dodged a bullet with that one. I'm not just saying this. I've seen those eyes before. Like someone from a war zone. Or those wild cats you get in the park. They're great for keeping down the vermin but you have to watch yourself around them."

Beth said, "Something's definitely changed. You wonder how he'll fit back in. We work with that department all the time and the regular detectives look like TV preachers."

"The big question is, did you get what you needed tonight?"

"What did I need?"

"Closure."

By way of an answer, she hugged him close.

He said over her shoulder, "Your ex is weird. I'm calling that a win."

The sex that followed was exceptional.

AFTERWARDS, AS they lay there in comfortable silence, Beth suddenly said, "What do you say we introduce him to Rebecca? She's single again."

Rick had been drifting away, but from the sound of it Beth was wide awake. Reluctantly, he roused himself to a response.

"Rebecca's *always* single," he said. "It's because she's such a flake."

"That's not fair."

"May not be fair, but it's true. The man's barely been home five minutes, let him take a breath."

"I guess."

"Mikey's called in sick," he added, by way of a hint. "If they can't find anyone else I may have to pull a double shift tomorrow."

But already Beth was back on topic. "Do you think he'd like Lauren?"

"All the guys like Lauren. Mostly because Lauren likes anyone with a functioning dick. Beth, if it's true, and he's been living the life of a fucking superspy for half a decade, do you really think there's no way that he can attract a woman without your help?"

There was a pause and then Beth said, warily, "Should I stop?"

"Just leave it be."

"I'll do that," she said, and all went quiet.

Rick tried again to sleep. But now he felt a vague discontent that he couldn't explain. He was all for Beth's repositioning of her old lover into the friend zone. But this, now?

He wasn't a jealous person.

But he could see how a jealous person might feel.

13

AFTER THE UBER dropped him at the curb, Danny walked up the driveway past the old Buick to reach the house. There was a garage, but the garage was a workshop. The old man had told Danny that he could borrow the Buick any time, but Danny was now thinking that he'd check for upcoming police auctions. Sometimes you could pick up a decent seizure vehicle for not much money, bidding against used car dealers who'd set a limit on their spend.

His dad had left a light on, just a low one in the kitchen. The dog didn't get out of his bed but his tail thumped on the floor a few times. Danny went to get some iced water from the chiller. The missed call light on the wall phone caught his eye. As the glass filled his father appeared in the doorway, hair awry, tying the cord on his dressing gown.

Danny said, "Did I wake you?"

"I don't sleep much these days," Joe said. "How's Beth?"

"Fine. She mentioned you. When did you see her?"

"Couple of times early on. She was pretty upset. There wasn't much we could say to her."

"She's a city hall lawyer now."

"Paralegal's what I heard. Good to know she bounced back."

"From what?"

"She had some kind of an episode. Took her out of law school for a year. Did she not say anything?"

"Not about that."

"And what about you?"

"What about me?"

"Come on, Danny."

"Water under the bridge, Dad. She's good, I'm good. I'm not saying it was easy but we've both had time to be over it."

Joe's look suggested that he wasn't quite buying that. Danny said, "Did you miss a call?" and gestured in the direction of the wall phone.

"Oh, that," Joe said, turning to look. He reached to clear off the light. "I get those all the time. If they don't leave a message you know they're trying to sell you something."

"Get a cell phone," Danny said.

"Got one."

"Then where is it?"

"I keep it switched off. It saves the battery."

Joe let the dog out into the yard for a late pee and Danny headed to his room. Another good reason for getting a car of his own; if you sat in the Buick for any length of time, you came out wearing an extra coat of Rufus.

He set the half-finished glass of water on the bedside table, kicked off his boots, and stretched out on the bed.

He'd lied to Joe. Having the time to be over something wasn't the same as being over it. The entire evening had been a low-level torment, steady and ever-present like a second-degree burn that never healed. He was a visiting stranger in the life that should have been his. Rick was a good man and that made it worse. Behind it all was the dread that wouldn't yield to logic, that wouldn't quite go away.

That vision, the hospital commissary. Pete Krikorian with his hand on Beth's shoulder.

Damaged Danny, making ghosts.

The trust was real, he'd told Simone Ali. *You know it's the job but you still come out feeling like Judas.*

Maybe there was nothing in it, and his therapist was right. There really were no ghosts, just haunted people.

While it might be true, it didn't help.

14

FOR RHIANNA IT had been a question of waiting for the right moment. The moment came with an instruction to bring in a hot weapon and a substantial package of cash from the boys in the Inland Empire. She headed over there and made the collection, placed the gun and the bag of money in the trunk of the Hyundai, and that same morning turned her aunt's car east and started to drive. No message, no goodbyes. In Barstow she stopped to pick up some warm clothing and a couple of packs of underwear. Her only other stop on that first day was for gas.

She had at least five thousand dollars in used bills. Didn't bother to count it, didn't care as long as it would cover her immediate needs. She could have made the journey by air, but that would have meant showing ID for a ticket and maybe questions at the airport over a baggage check. Even if she could get by with the money, she'd have to forego the firearm and that was too good a gift to pass up.

She needed to keep her profile low. The organisation might be in disarray, but going rogue with gang funds was still a punishable offence. No matter that she was on a mission for Armen. No matter that she was hunting down their witness. Soldiers like Rhianna were for scut work and admin. This was the stage of the exercise she wouldn't be trusted for. Closing the job would be handed to one of the guys, despite their consistent record of screwing up.

The simple fact was, she wasn't doing it for Armen.

The distance from coast to coast was close to three thousand miles. At first she reckoned she could make it in a week or less, but even before the first day was out she realised that she was greatly overestimating her capacity for long hours of driving. East of Joseph City she zoned out at the wheel and almost ran off the road. She left the freeway at Holbrook where she checked into an Econo Lodge, sleeping until housekeeping woke her late the next morning.

After that she settled into a rhythm. She slept in budget motels, lived off pancakes and bacon and gallons of coffee in diners and truck stops where she sat alone and no one ever approached or bothered her. Sometimes as she drove Nico rode alongside her. She had a powerful sense of his presence, just beyond the corner of her eye. She never looked his way. She knew that if she looked, he'd be gone.

Passing the sign for Cuervo, the low fuel warning light started to show. There were other warning lights on the dash as well, but she'd been ignoring those. She took the exit onto a road that ran on alongside the highway to a red dirt ghost town, a loose collection of mostly abandoned ruins scattered widely across the New Mexico desert.

At Cuervo Gas she filled the tank, and before she'd gone a hundred yards from the pumps her aunt's car died. The noises it made when she tried to restart were enough to convince her that its condition truly was terminal. The fuel she'd just put in the tank was now worth more than the vehicle.

Rhianna took her clothes and bag of money from the trunk and abandoned the car by the roadside, leaving it slowly cooling over a pool of dirty oil. She put the keys through the door of Tony's Wrecker Service and set out to hitch hike to Amarillo.

Hitching was more hazardous than driving, especially for a young woman travelling alone. In the restroom of a Chester's Chicken she took the precaution of taping the remaining money to her body, as much of it as would fit under her clothing. The firearm went into the lining of her coat. She felt no guilt over the cash or the car, and gave no thought to those she'd left behind. They didn't exist for her now. Her life was pure, her purpose clear.

In Memphis she boarded a bus. Between Memphis and Atlanta a fellow passenger sold her some pills, to which she reacted badly. At 3 a.m. in the Greyhound Station on Forsyth Street, midway through the hours-long wait for a transfer and unable to settle on a hard metal bench worn down to the primer, she began to believe that her mind was growing sharper than it had ever been before. She left her body and soared above her surroundings. She held the universe within her.

Someone had to shake her into consciousness when her departure was called.

The bag with her clothes was gone but her money was safe, what was left of it, wrapped tight to her body under her shirt. The handgun was still in the lining of her coat. The burner phone was in one pocket, the SIM card in another. They were all that mattered. The phone was her compass, her lifeline. Both her future and her past.

Her journey was far from over, but its destination was never far from her mind.

She burned with her purpose. Or the fever of exhaustion. It was hard to tell.

15

T WAS THE start of a new week and Danny was still looking to link a name to his homeless victim. He was going through a backlog of Missing Persons when he was called into Captain Connor's office. The chief was there. He'd dropped by to shake Danny's hand and thank him for his service, which was awkward. There were no cameras for obvious reasons, so the chief didn't stay for more than a few minutes. Afterwards Danny spent an hour on the range in the basement, where he learned from retired Sergeant Tony Mendoza that everything he knew about handling guns was wrong.

There was a small park across the street from the Hall of Justice. He walked over to sit on a bench, watch the squirrels, and make a call.

"Beth's got a new guy," he told Vince.

"Like you thought that wouldn't happen."

"I knew it would happen. Or a part of me knew. You wouldn't think I'd be this far down the line and still care."

"We all have those thoughts. She's the path not taken, Danny. If it wasn't her it would be someone else."

"I may have messed up her life. I think I'm the reason she dropped out of school."

"Danny..."

"She was the one with the shining future, Vince. You want to see where she's living."

"Danny. In all the years undercover I never had to say this to you, but I'm saying it now. Get a grip."

"Yeah, you're right."

"Take up a sport. Join a book club."

"Now there's a thought," Danny said.

HE'D NO actual intention of joining a book club, but Vince had given him an idea. The George W. Franklin Library was only two blocks away. A couple of hours later he was back, and making his way across the building to Room 235. Victim Support shared office space with Special Prosecutions which was a department of the county attorney's office, one floor up and not unlike the department he'd just left. Also open-plan with no reception desk, but everyone present and busy. As Danny ventured in a youngish sandy-haired man rose and said, "Can I help you?"

This was Bob, he supposed. Danny said, "Looking for Beth Franklin?"

He'd already spotted her. Three desks away, standing with her back to them, consulting with a coworker while they scrolled through some document online. She turned at the sound of her name. Without letting go of the box he was holding, Danny signalled a greeting.

She came over, clearly wondering why he was here, and they moved to a quietish spot while he explained.

"They fenced off the library while they strip out the fixtures but I spoke to Norah, she's the head librarian. They've kept her on while they break up the collection. They've been selling off the books for a dollar a box and what didn't sell went into a dumpster. She said she was physically sick, had to stay home that day. But she saved these."

Beth lifted one of the leather-bound volumes from the box. She opened the book with care.

Danny said, "They have your grandfather's personal bookplate."

"Great-grandfather," Beth said, absently, as she turned the pages.

"She said they had an entire founders' collection. But over the years…"

"I know."

"The valuable stuff went first."

"Wow," she said. "Danny… I don't know what to say."

"Thank Norah. All I did was ask. I wanted to… I don't know. Make some kind of amends. I was hoping there might be more. After I talked to my dad last night I began to understand what I'd put you through."

"I may have had my issues," she said. "I'm over them. Let's leave it at that."

He felt his phone buzz in his pocket. He said to Beth, "Excuse me," and turned away to take the call.

It was Detective Ericsson. He said, "Hey, Danny? Pick up your messages. One of your pawnbrokers got a bite."

AS DANNY let himself in from the street he heard from deep in the store, "*Don't you try to scam me, Apu, I brought you a genuine Rolex.*"

Of the pawnbrokers in town, Benji's Pawn and Gun was the one with the slogan *Never Pay Retail*. Benji's was a deep, narrow space with a strongroom at the back and a teller's booth for gold appraisal. One wall was all guitars and memorabilia, another carried a long rack of shotguns and rifles. Manager Chris was Indian and in his thirties. He wore a sharp suit and a necktie to work every day. Before him stood a young guy making impatient noises over a counter where knives, chains, rings and watches were on show under glass.

Danny closed the door behind himself and moved forward. "Maybe I can be of help," he said.

The young man looked back. Early twenties, angular, not well cared for. Danny recognised him. He'd been talking to Beth at the bus camp. The cast on his hand and wrist was grubby and frayed and his shirt sleeve had been slit back to fit over it.

"Stay out of this," the young man said.

"I'm no appraiser but I can claim some expertise, here," Danny said. "I've lived in a city where muggers gather high-end watches like fruit pickers in high season. The stupid ones try to pawn them."

In an instant the young man slammed his cast down onto the glass display. The glass was tough but it wasn't shatterproof, and it went with a bang. He reached in with his good hand and grabbed the biggest hunting knife of the set, whirling to face Danny with it.

"Get out of my way," he said.

THE NEXT THING YOU SEE WHEN YOU DIE

"Or what?"

"Or I'll shred you up right here."

Danny was unperturbed. He made a once-over assessment of the Wiry Young Man, standing there in his confrontational pose, and then spoke past him to the manager.

"Hey, Chris," he said. "It *is* Chris, isn't it? Toss me the Sandberg?"

Chris the pawn shop guy looked behind him, and then took an autographed baseball bat from where it rested across two clips on the wall. He threw it to Danny, who caught it by the handle and in the same smooth move brought it down hard and smacked the knife right out of the young man's good hand. The boy yelled in pain.

"Strike one," said Danny.

With the end of the bat, Danny poked him in the gut just enough to wind him.

"And two," he said.

Danny laid the bat on the counter and took the incapacitated thief by the collar. As they moved toward the door, Danny said, "You have the right to remain silent."

Wheezing. "You're a cop?"

"Pay attention. Anything you say can and will be used against you in a court of law…"

That was all he could remember, but help was at hand.

"He has the right to an attorney," Chris called after them.

"You have a right to an attorney."

"'If you cannot afford an attorney, one will be appointed for you.'"

"Okay," Danny said, "I've got it now."

They'd reached the door,

"No hablo Inglese," the young guy gasped.

"Yeah," Danny said. "Good one."

WHEN BELINDA Lee got back to the office it was to find Danny sitting with his ass hitched onto a desk and holding forth to an audience comprising Detectives Beaman and Ericsson, Bola the civilian clerk, and some rando who'd been delivering a refill for the water cooler. Danny was holding up the contested wristwatch in a clear evidence bag.

She stopped, taking in the scene.

"Couple of years ago I had to move a thousand fake Rolexes," Danny was saying. "A deal had gone wrong and that was all the guy could offer in payment. We took the watches and broke his legs and called it square. What I learned was that a genuine Rolex has two numbers, a serial number and a case reference number."

Beaman said, "You broke his legs?"

"Not personally. But he agreed the deal and showed up for it. Different world. Anyway, this is an Oyster Perpetual. Worn by someone who likes quality but isn't a showoff. Timothy Dalton has one."

Water cooler guy, who looked about sixteen, said, "Who?"

"Timothy Dalton? James Bond?"

Nope, nothing. Continue. Danny now expanded his reach to include Belinda Lee in the circle. "Rolex don't keep customer records but if your victim ever had it serviced around here, there's a chance he'll be in the watchmaker's files. If it belonged to our down-on-his-luck dead guy, then we may be able to give him a name. And if the stains on that surgical cast show the victim's DNA then we've got his killer as well."

Belinda Lee said, "If I can interrupt the lap of honor, your father has been trying to get hold of you."

"Excuse me," Danny said, and moved away to make the call. "Thanks," he said.

Detective Lee said, "Leave the watch."

Out of earshot of the others, he called the house.

Joe came right in with, "Did you take the car this morning?"

"I took the bus," Danny said. "I told you."

"Well, someone's had it."

"What do you mean?"

"If it wasn't you then someone stole the car from the driveway. I just had a call from your people to say it's been found."

"When?"

"Just now. Must have been taken some time this morning."

"You didn't notice it was gone?"

"I thought you had it! They said if I don't pick it up, it's going to be towed."

"How did this happen? Don't you keep it locked?"

"Can't say for sure."

"Do you even take the keys out?"

"Come on," Joe said. "Who'd steal a fifteen-year-old Buick?"

There was an obvious reply, for which Danny couldn't even summon the energy. Joe added, "If they tow it, she said that's going to cost me money."

"What do you want me to do, Dad?"

"Nothing. Just telling you."

There was a silence. Then Danny gave in and said, wearily, "Okay, where is it?"

16

HE KNEW THE location, the truss bridge at Cooper Creek upstream from the Cooper Creek Mall. Detective Beaman offered him a ride out and dropped him by a crossroads above the creek. From here a foot trail cut down through woodland to join up with the gravel way. Beaman's generosity didn't extend to busting a spring in his personal vehicle on a dirt road that had been let to ruin so Danny waved his thanks and made his way down alone, pushing aside branches and stepping over roots.

The bridge had been a regular teen hangout place, once. He'd been this way before but not in ten, twelve years. When they built the mall in the nineties they extended the highway to deal with the new traffic. They closed the old bridge and the single-track mine road fell out of use. The creek had been an occasional swimming spot until a boy drowned there in 2005. The Buick wouldn't be the first car abandoned in the area, but why? Most stolen cars were high-value models worth the effort of cracking their security. Either that, or they were older cars easier to lift for one-off use in a crime. There had been no robberies reported, nothing that called for the use of a stolen vehicle. Taking an old man's car from outside his house and then running it down a remote dead end just to dump it—he could imagine no motive other than mischief for mischief's sake.

Jesus, they hadn't just run the car down to the end of the trail, they'd driven it right out onto the bridge and left it there. The official barrier had been nothing more than a couple of crossed planks, rotted and busted, and they'd easily been kicked down. The platform timbers of the bridge itself were much heftier but they were also close to a hundred years old, and it would have been no great surprise if the Buick had rolled out to the middle and plunged straight through.

The creek below was high and racing, just as it had been back when Nathan Gibbons drowned. Danny stepped over the fallen barrier and made his way out with care. The timbers underfoot bore a coat of slime and the iron framework of the structure was so decayed that the trusses were more rust than metal. He'd need to take care when backing the car off, assuming the thieves hadn't blown up the engine.

If they'd ditched the keys he'd have a problem. It was a simple ignition but hotwiring wasn't his forte. He'd seen it done, never done one himself.

Below him, the waters roared. The bridge was barely more than a single vehicle's width and he had to turn sideways and slide along the car to reach the windshield, where a police notice had been plastered onto the glass. He reached over to tear it off.

Then stopped.

This was no notice. It was a sheet of letter paper pinned under the wipers. It hadn't stayed flat, but had folded back in a flap to show a list made with a Sharpie by some careful hand.

Four names.

Reuben, shot five times and never had a chance.

Pete Kricorian, stabbed in prison.

Anita, who took her own life.

And printed bigger than the others, Nico.

And now there was something cold and metal pushing up against his cheek.

"You were supposed to get in the car, *then* see them."

Danny was very still. He could see himself reflected, he could see the gun at his head, and he could see the young woman holding it. He just hadn't seen it coming.

He said, "I'm going to turn around."

Rhianna said, "No, you're not," but Danny spun around so fast that she didn't have a chance to react. With his left he grabbed her gun hand and kept it high and pointed away. With his right he caught her neck and propelled her into the guardrail.

The guardrail was only partial here. Some plastic tape had once been strung across the gaps, now serving no real purpose.

Rhianna was teetering back with the water rushing a dozen yards below. Only Danny's grip and the rusty rail were keeping her from falling.

With a nod toward the gun he said, "You drop it, or I drop you."

"Then what?" Defiance all the way, and not a trace of fear.

Danny studied her for a few moments and then said, "What do you want me to say, Rhianna? It was never personal."

She spat in his face.

She wasn't letting go of the gun. He could hold it pointed away but as long as they were like this he couldn't risk trying to take it from her.

He said, "Who else knows I'm here?"

She wouldn't answer. For a fraction of a second Danny made as if to let her fall, with the intention of shaking her up.

It didn't work.

She said, "Nice try. But I know you. You never do your killing face-to-face."

"Unlike you?"

"I don't want you dead. I want you to suffer."

"So how was that gonna work? It's not even my car."

"You weren't supposed be the one who showed up."

Danny didn't get it for a moment.

Then he did.

He said, "You weren't expecting me. You were going for my dad."

Poised over the water, Rhianna began to grin.

Danny's next move was so fast that it took even him by surprise. He abruptly released Rhianna's gun hand and with his other gave her a hard shove in the chest, toppling her backward. The guardrail gave way and she went through it with an astonished look on her face. She dropped away from him, down, down toward the river in free fall, the handgun floating away through the air as she let it go.

She hit the moving water like a sheet of steel and when the spray of her impact finally fell, there was nothing.

Danny was still on the same spot, staring down in disbelief. What the fuck did he just do?

The water rushed on under, deep and deadly.

He saw no sign of Rhianna at all.

She was gone. The gun was gone. It was as if neither had ever been there. He couldn't believe it. He re-ran the moment, questioning whether it had even happened. But there was the rail, bent out. There was the plastic tape, ripped and fluttering.

And there was the river, pitiless and fast.

He leaned back against the car.

Whatever he'd done, there was no going back. Then Danny Undercover kicked in. His mind started to work again and he glanced all around. Witnesses? Cameras?

Nothing in any direction. She'd chosen the spot well.

He turned to the Buick. Pulled the handbill from under the wiper and stuffed it in his pocket. Opened the door and slid into the driver seat. What was her plan? Explain to Joe what his son had done to her life and then—what?

He hardly had to guess. A rickety bridge and a dangerous river. She'd not just chosen well, she'd chosen for a purpose.

He steepled his hands and covered his face for a few moments, until his breathing steadied and he got a grip on his racing emotions.

She hadn't used keys. There was a screwdriver jammed into the ignition lock and she'd used that.

Focused and under control, he turned the screwdriver and started the engine.

Old timbers creaked under the tires as he inched the car backwards off the bridge, but they held. Once safely on land he took another moment to gather himself, then left the engine running while he got out and checked that part of the bridge for anything left behind. He bent the guardrail into roughly its old position. Back in the driver's seat he swung the car about, ready to pick up the dirt road back to the highway.

He put behind him the silence of the valley.

He put behind him the waters of the river, flowing fast and deep.

SO MUCH for an anonymous return to his old life. If Rhianna could find him, so could others. He didn't know whether there'd been a leak by the justice system, or information passed on by a corrupt insider—a real irony there, if the gang had someone undercover in the LAPD—or if some error of his own had created a trail for her to follow. The point was that his entire world here stood exposed. His fear of bringing trouble home had been justified, but not in the way he'd imagined.

There was also the fact that he'd just pitched a young woman into a raging torrent like a sackful of rocks. But that wasn't troubling him as much as it should.

For all its age the Buick still had some power, and once he hit the highway he opened up. Some fifteen minutes later he was braking to a halt on the street outside his father's house. There was already a vehicle in the driveway, a shiny new pickup pulled in as bold as anything. The sight of it increased Danny's concern. He jumped out of the car and headed for the door.

Instead of entering he stopped, he listened. Then he made his way around to the back of the house, moving like a thief. The kitchen window was slightly open. He listened again and there was no sound.

He'd no weapon. He looked around and saw nothing he could use. He wished he'd yanked the screwdriver out of the car. He slipped his hand into his pocket and improvised a makeshift knuckleduster out of his house keys.

Free hand on the handle, count, go.

He burst in. And found Joe sitting there, reading a truck brochure with Rufus at his feet. He didn't seem surprised.

"Heard you pull in," Joe said. "Thanks for getting the car. Anything to say who took it?"

Danny took a moment.

Then he said, "Whose is the truck?"

"It's on tryout. Been thinking about it anyway, and this seemed like a sign. I had them drop it off this morning. If I decide to buy it you can keep the Buick."

Danny quietly pocketed his house keys, and made an effort to appear calm. Then he moved to the window.

"Sure," he said, closing and locking the window. "Because every young single guy needs a seniors' car."

"You're not so young, and it's a gift, so shut your hole."

"Keep the locks on, dad. Anyone could walk in here."

Joe used the brochure to indicate Rufus. "Got my guard dog," he said.

"I mean it."

Danny moved through into the main room. He checked the patio doors and found them also unsecured, to let the dog come and go. As he was making them fast Joe moved to stand in the doorway to the kitchen. This was serious now, and Joe had sensed it.

He said, "What's the matter, son?"

Danny said, "Probably nothing, Dad. But we need to be careful for a while. Who told you the car had been found?"

"Some woman from the highways department. Left me a message."

"Is it still on there?"

Joe played it. Rhianna, for sure. He could think of only one way she might have discovered the number, and that was through his burner. Investigators hadn't found it. He wasn't even sure they'd looked too hard.

Why hadn't he seen it? For a car to be taken, dumped, discovered, reported, and the owner contacted…nothing happened that fast. Danny Undercover would have been suspicious. Danny Kasabian needed to raise his game.

With the house locked down Danny went out onto the lawn, out of his father's earshot, to make a call. He kept his voice low to avoid an overshare with the neighbors.

He said, "She found me through the phone, Vince. Who else is gonna show up?"

"I'll see what I can find out," Vince said. "Where is she now?"
There was a pause.
Then Danny said, "Dealt with."
"Danny?" Vince said. "What did you do? Danny?"
Danny ended the call.

17

THE RIVER WAS wide and shallow here, and ran slow. The late summer drought had yet to kick in but already the mudflats were appearing, drawing in hordes of sandpipers and a variety of other shorebirds. In less than a mile the river would narrow again to create a set of ferocious rapids. Along with some old mine pollution, these had doomed local efforts to create a Cooper Creek paddle trail.

From the mud of the riverbank, a filthy figure levered itself up like a golem separating from the earth. She had no sense where she was. She had no sense of how far along she'd come. She'd survived on scant gasps of air in those brief moments when the current had spun her up to the surface. Though she was out of the water, she was still in danger of drowning. Thick mud filled her nose, her mouth, her eyes, it plastered her hair to her head and her clothes to her body. When she breathed in, she inhaled it.

She snorted out mud and mucous so hard that she'd have sworn that brain matter was coming out with it. Before rising fully she scooped up a handful of the river and tried to swill her face clear. But it was still foul.

She balanced unsteadily on her feet, and then started to pick her way to firmer ground. She'd lost a shoe. When she reached grass, she sat. Right then she couldn't have said who she was, let alone how she came to be here. It was as if she'd crawled out of the slime like a whole new species.

A few yards downriver there was a wide drainage pipe emptying into the stream. She hitched herself along to it. The wastewater wasn't clean, but it was cleaner than her. She washed off what she could.

Then she threw up all the river that she'd swallowed.

Rhianna was exhausted, disoriented. Her head sang, like a whispering of many voices.

But she had to move. She rose, and somehow found the strength to ascend the bank. As she reached the top, it came into view; a shining city, all laid out before her. Only a raggedy hurricane fence, seven feet high, stood between them. Where hurricane wire met concrete pillar, a triangular section of it had been peeled back to create a secret gateway to a promised land.

The promised land's parking lot was vast and mostly empty, its few cars gathered by the limited number of building entrances. Out here at the extremities, weeds were pushing up through the asphalt. Cooper Creek Mall was neither big nor busy. Clothes ruined, caked in mud, streaked with river dirt and terrifying to behold, a dishevelled Rhianna Madisson shambled across the wide and barren lot, heading for a central portico with fake concrete pillars and a Delphic temple design whose classical roots were entirely in the mind of its Charlotte-based architect.

The doors opened at her approach, and she walked in. Once inside, she paused for a moment and looked around. The sound system was playing Elvis. Two levels, and a high glass arcade roof. The mall had struggled from the beginning; some of the shuttered units had never been occupied. Sears had pulled out a couple of years before, leaving Cooper Creek with no anchor store and a long, slow slide to dead mall status.

A couple on their way out gave her a quizzical look, but she ignored them. She'd seen a drinking fountain against the wall. She went straight over to it and hit and held the button. Water bubbled up and she bent over it, drinking greedily. Unlike the river, it was clean; and though it would be a stretch of the imagination to call it sweet, it was welcome.

She drank until she was bloated and then she straightened, wiping her mouth with her forearm. This left her with a half-cleaned streak from elbow to wrist. She stared at this dirt track for a moment and then looked around for a store guide.

By the time the mall guards reached the fountain, she was elsewhere.

The women's restroom was spotless and unoccupied. A row of empty cubicles to her left, a row of basins and mirrors to her right. On the way to the basins she pulled a handful of paper towels from a dispenser.

At the second basin in she started the hot water running and began to clean herself up. The water ran for less than thirty seconds and then shut itself off, so she had to keep hitting the button. On the dirt, she was barely making an impression. The towels quickly became unusable and she had to get more. She'd caught sight of herself in the mirror on the way in, and she was trying not to look again. But the mirrors ran the entire length of the room, and the Rhianna in the mirror was hard to avoid.

Without thinking, she glanced up.

Ho. Lee. Shit.

In the room, she was alone.

But in the mirror, she was not.

All four of them were there. As if in the room behind her. She turned to look and there was no one. She turned back to the mirror, expecting them to be gone, and there they were still. Reuben, shot five times by the cops and bleeding from his wounds. Pete Kricorian, stabbed in jail. It played like a mantra in her mind now. Anita, the middle-aged mother who took her own life; Anita was closest to her in the reflection, right behind her shoulder.

And Nico? Where was Nico?

Anita spoke.

"*Rhianna,*" she said. "*We got work to do.*"

The voice was in her head, not in the room, but Rhianna wasn't listening to her. She was looking past the older woman, looking for Nico. Was he there? That shadow, facing away? She was willing him to turn and see so that he could understand the depth of her love. If only he would turn. Their eyes would meet. The veil between life and death would fall.

Anita said, "*Nico has nothing to say to you.*"

THE NEXT THING YOU SEE WHEN YOU DIE

It was unfair. She was loyal. See what she'd done, how far she'd travelled. But all that seemed to matter was that she'd failed. Again she willed Nico to turn, with no effect. She began to speak his name.

And at that moment, the door flew open and two mall cops burst in, both male.

They'd been knocking and calling. Rhianna had heard none of it. They were speaking to her now but she didn't take it in. They were a distraction she didn't want and their sudden presence made it even more urgent that she got Nico's attention, but when she went back to the mirror it was to find the spell broken and the figures all gone.

She flew at the two guards, a whirlwind of fury. They weren't expecting anything like it, and threw up their hands to protect their heads and faces in a pussy move that would later make them grateful for the absence of restroom cameras. They weren't armed but they had shock batons on their belts, and no chance to reach for them; it only ended when one of them blindly managed to hook a foot behind Rhianna's ankle and take her legs out from under her. There was a loud crack as the back of her head clipped a basin on the way down; it was a glancing connection, maybe not hard enough to do serious damage, but certainly sufficient to knock the fight out of her.

She wasn't moving now. The two guards shared a queasy look as she lay there. This could have repercussions. One of them quickly checked along the cubicles but all the doors were open, so no witnesses. The other one crouched and lightly slapped Rhianna's cheek, the way all good first responders don't.

"Hey," he said. "Hey, miss. Wake up."

Her eyes half-opened.

"Let's get her out," the first one said.

They took an arm each and hauled her to her feet. There wasn't much weight to her, and it wasn't hard. The handsy one said, "Can you walk?" and took her lack of response for a yes. "Come on," he said. "Let's walk."

Their aim was just to get her to the exit and out into the world. She'd committed no crime other than that of being an unsightly presence in a public place. Despite all her cleanup efforts she still resembled a one-shoed scarecrow dipped in tar.

They walked her out. The restrooms were up on the gallery floor and they headed for the escalators. She was still damp, still rank. Each did his best to hold her at a distance. As they moved, Rhianna's head began to clear.

Clarity being a relative term.

Those people who were passing and those who were stopping to watch, she could see right through them. Real people, ordinary people, and it was as if they were translucent. Ghosts, even. Only one solid figure stood out. That was Anita on the gallery opposite, silently watching as they marched Rhianna away, her head slowly turning to follow.

On the escalator, descending, she could see down into the lower level. More people there, thin and pale as water, apart from two. The solid presences were Reuben, over by the kiddie rides, and Pete Kricorian, by a shuttered branch of Pretzel Twister. They were her reality now, the rest of passing humanity no more than shapes cut out of mist. Only one was missing.

Rhianna held herself in terror. A grip so tight it could be taken for calm. Where was Nico? She looked back. There was a figure at the top of the escalator far behind them, looking down.

She tried to speak his name, and one of the mall cops said, "There's nothing here for you," and they continued to propel her forward as they reached ground level.

It was overwhelming. Her world was spinning and her head was about to explode. She couldn't stand it any longer.

Her hands flew out to either side. Neither man was expecting it. She grasped and yanked the stun gun from each man's belt and before they could react she jammed both weapons against her own head, one to each temple, and fired them off.

Pow.

Darkness. Relief.

18

IT WASN'T EASY. But Danny had to focus on the day job.

The watchmaker enquiries paid off with a name that matched up with a missing persons report from two years before, Michael James Swanwick. He'd once hit and killed a child with his car. He wasn't drunk, he wasn't blamed. But what followed was a history of failing business and mental breakdown, a walkout from the family home, a refusal of all help and a descent into a solitary life on the margins of society. His wife—widow, now—had seen him once, washing car windows with a broken squeegee for coins; when she stopped and got out and called to him he'd fled, refusing even to look back at her. After she reported the sighting he technically wasn't a missing person, simply a man who'd made his choices. She'd heard nothing of him since.

Danny went to her home to break the news and was accompanied by one of Beth's colleagues, who stayed behind to offer support. He'd wondered if Beth might show up for the job. But maybe she'd heard mention of Danny's name, and chosen to pass.

No matter, now. He'd struggled through the day and he'd come to his decision.

When he went to return the file to Belinda Lee's desk, she got to him first.

She said, "Did you go to the family?"

"Yes."

"That was for me to handle."

"You weren't interested when you thought it was nobody."

"Well I'm interested now," she said. She snatched the file from him and stomped off in a mood.

Danny called after, "There's no such thing as a nobody."

She spun around and came back, and got right into his face.

"Just who do you think you are?" she said. "I respect your undercover work but I've got no respect for you as a cop, because you aren't one. Dealing drugs and breaking legs and sleeping with gang whores qualifies you for nothing around here. I let you play detective. My mistake. Now it's gonna bite me in the ass. Happy?"

"Not happy, no. I'm quitting."

"Oh?"

"I'm compromised here, Belinda. They know where I am."

She adjusted to this new information. "Says who?"

He didn't want to go into details. "I could stick around for the old man's sake but it's not just him. If I don't leave I'll be putting a lot of people at risk."

"Like Beth Franklin."

That was not expected. He said, "What do you mean?"

"Come on, Danny," she said. "It's a small town. Norah's in my book group."

"So give me a better reason. Can you ask them to get the paperwork together? And I'll need whatever I'm owed."

"If it's what you want."

"It's what I want."

Her anger defused, she made a helpless gesture of regret. "You're a work in progress, Danny," she said. "But we could have figured this out."

"I appreciate the thought," he said. "Thanks, Belinda."

19

SHOWERED AND CLEAN, in patient-issue clothing and slippers, Rhianna sat in the interview room with her hands folded in her lap and waited for her second evaluation. They called it light security, but it still meant locked doors. One of the ER clinicians had filed an emergency petition and she'd been transported to this psychiatric facility on a seventy-two-hour hold.

She was a proven danger to herself, if not to others. She'd slept off the sedation in a resident room with walls the color of desert sand and sheets of dusty blue. Nature colors, chosen for calm. It was her best sleep in ages, deep and dreamless. Drugs were great.

This conversation would determine whether she was fit for release. If the judgment was no she'd get a hearing before a district judge within the next ten days. It would mean being detained at least until then.

Her doctor entered the room, gave her a brief smile, and laid her file notes on the table as he moved around it to sit facing her.

He said, "Rhianna. Are you ready to carry on?"

She reckoned he was in his forties, maybe a little older. On first impression, somewhat rumpled and likeable.

Rhianna said, "I didn't hurt anyone."

"I know."

"So when can I leave?"

"Not just yet."

"What am I accused of?"

"This isn't a prison," he said. "You're accused of nothing. You're here for your own protection."

"I wasn't trying to kill myself," Rhianna said. "That would make it too easy for certain people."

"What people are those?"

At this point she realised how she needed to step carefully. Say too little and she wouldn't help herself. Give away too much and she'd expose her mission. Tell the whole truth and they'd lock her up for good. That wouldn't just mean consequences for her, but also blowback on Armen and the others.

He tried another tack. "So what were you doing?"

"I needed to clear my head."

"With two tasers."

"That was a little extreme," she admitted.

"Did the voices stop?"

Rhianna looked away and offered no answer. She'd made the mistake of mentioning the voices in her first evaluation, when she'd been drowsy and drugged and her thoughts were still disordered from the self-administered shock treatment. The danger now was that her remarks would be taken as a sign of paranoia, or delusion, or worse.

He pressed her. "What do they tell you?"

She looked at him then, wanting him to understand. She said, "They're not those kind of voices. I'm not one of your crazies."

"Okay."

And then, unable to help herself, she said, "They're dead people. With a grievance."

He nodded as if this was entirely reasonable. He said, "Do you only hear them? Or do you also see them?"

"I see them sometimes," she said, then corrected herself. "Once. I saw them once."

He indicated around the room. "Do you see them now?"

Rhianna snorted, as if that was a ridiculous suggestion. "Do you?" she said.

Again he nodded, as if this was the most sensible of replies, and started to write something on his file notes. She leaned forward slightly, trying not to make it obvious that she was looking, but she couldn't read what it was.

He didn't seem to mind her seeing anyway. He said, "You're going to be with us for a little while, Rhianna. A last name would be useful."

Without being unpleasant about it, Rhianna remained unforthcoming.

He said, "I'd like to be able to contact your family."

Again, silence from her.

He sighed and said, "All right, then, Rhianna, but it doesn't make it easy for either one of us."

Rhianna made a slight shrug of apology. He seemed a decent person. She felt sorry for him.

He laid down the pen and gathered his notes. "Someone will take you to your room," he said.

"No need," Rhianna said.

His hand was braced on the table as he started to rise. She picked up his pen and slammed it down hard on the web between his fingers and thumb, pinning his hand to the table. He gasped in surprise and disbelief. Before he could make any further sound, Rhianna moved around behind him and slid her arm around his neck. Gripping her wrist with her other hand to apply pressure, she began to choke him unconscious.

"Hey," she said. "Come on. Sleep, now."

She's done it to a school friend once, to end an argument. It had caused her a lot of trouble then. But the experience was paying off now.

When she was sure he'd gone, she propped him upright and went through his pockets. There was a TV eye high in the corner of the room, but there'd be many such cameras and someone had to be watching the right screen at the right moment to catch a transgression. Stay calm, move slowly, don't draw the eye. She took his cash, his credit cards, and the swipe card that would get her through certain doors. Others opened by numeric keypads but she'd noted and memorised those she'd passed through. The staff escorting her hadn't made much effort to conceal what they were doing.

He started to stir. She put him down again.

He'd raise the alarm as soon as he was conscious. That would only be a couple of minutes so she'd have to move. She picked up the file of notes and tucked it under her arm. She left his phone;

it might have live tracking activated. There'd be more cameras along the way but the trick was to ignore them. Confidence creates doubt, doubt buys you time, and by the time they respond you'll be gone. She'd a half-formed plan, but mostly she'd improvise.

Twenty minutes later a bus was braking to a halt on the street beside the hospital. A line of ancillary workers was waiting to board, their shift just ended. No one paid much attention to the young woman in the jogging pants and zip-up fleece.

Just another one of the cleaners.

20

WHEN HE CALLED Beth's direct number it went to voicemail. She got back to him late in the day, and he asked if they could meet. Same diner and, by coincidence, same booth. She was there already when he arrived.

As he slid into the bench he started it with, "Thanks for this. Busy time?"

Either she didn't hear the question or she ignored it. She said, "What's this about, Danny?"

Okay. Straight to it. He said, "Do you know people are talking about us? I want you to know it's not coming from me."

"Danny—"

"Before you say anything, I'm leaving town. So it won't be a problem. I'm sorry if it caused you one. I should never have come back. It's caused more trouble than I could have imagined."

She was blank.

"Fuck," she said.

"It was a mistake," he said. "Me thinking I could fit back in. You can see that, can't you? It's been too long. I'm different, you're different, everything changed."

"I don't get it," she said. "Where will you go?"

He could only shrug. "I don't know that yet."

She said, "Don't do this because of me."

"It's more than that. But you *are* a consideration. If I stay it's going to cause too many people too much pain. Don't worry about me. Don't think about me. And please don't ever try to find me."

The waitress came by then. Beth already had a Coke, Danny shook his head. The waitress moved on to the woman who'd just occupied the next booth.

When he returned his attention to Beth, she looked away. Her chin was trembling. He was shocked to see that her composure was about to go.

"Hey," he said, and moved to cover her hand with his own. She pulled hers away.

"Don't," she said. So he waited.

She got herself under control. Speaking carefully, she went on, "Understand this. I am over you. But these fucking scars. Scar tissue. That's what you left me with, Danny, and every time I think of us it pulls and it hurts."

"I'm sorry."

"I know."

"They swore to me they'd find you and explain."

"No one said a word."

"So this time it's coming from me. So you'll know. I won't pull the same stunt and just vanish on you twice. But I will find somewhere and disappear. New place, new person. I can do it. It's the one thing I do really well."

THE NEXT THING YOU SEE WHEN YOU DIE

He waited, but she didn't respond. He said, "Are you going to be okay?"

She took a deep breath and summoned herself as if for a leap and then said, "Don't go."

Danny was lost for a response.

"Please," she said at obvious cost. "Don't go."

"Okay," Danny said. "You need to understand this. Those people I got in with, the ones I betrayed. They know where I am. I'm a target now but it's not just me they'd be coming for. No one I love is safe."

The L word.

The world changer.

Her eyes met his. He stayed steady.

"This is so fucked up," she said.

"Let me deal with it," he said. "The only way I can see how."

"What happened out there, Danny? What happened to you?"

"I made people trust me. And then I ruined their lives. It's never going to happen again. You've got Rick. Rick's great. Look after each other. And forget about me. As of now. You can do it. Goodbye, Beth."

HE LEFT her there. She watched him all the way down the diner and he didn't look back. And she kept on watching him through the window as he climbed into a well-used old Buick. Joe's car, she remembered. He seemed to have some trouble getting started but then he pulled out of the parking spot and drove away.

She sat with her fist to her forehead, shaking her head.

The Coke went flat. Untouched.

Eventually, moving slowly, she gathered herself to leave. It took her two or three attempts to focus. She remembered to lay down some money for the check. It was as if she'd been knocked off the rails. It was taking an effort to set herself back on.

She rose to go. Before she'd taken more than a couple of steps she heard, "Don't leave without your phone."

She looked back. The woman in the next booth was leaning out, holding up a Samsung.

That can't be mine, Beth thought. *Mine's…* But as she felt in her coat pocket for it, she realised that it wasn't there.

"Thanks," she said, slightly bewildered, and went back to take it.

"You're welcome," the woman said. She was young. Her hair a home dye job with the roots now growing out. Jogging pants and a zip-up fleece.

"Beth, isn't it?" she said.

21

THEY'D TALKED UNTIL late and then Danny went to his room. Joe watched from the doorway as Danny was packing to go. Danny said, "If you meant it about keeping the car, I'll need the papers."

"On the table," Joe said. "What about money?"

"I've got some coming. You know I won't be able to call. It's not like before."

"But we'll get you back when the trial's all done."

"That's the idea," Danny lied.

The way he explained it to Joe, he'd be off the grid until after the sentencing. And while Danny could never be certain of what the future held, he knew that his private intentions were otherwise. There'd be no second homecoming. To those that Daniel Kasabian loved, and any he might grow to love, he risked being forever a toxic presence. He might yet live a life. But it wouldn't be this one.

He went into the kitchen to pick up the papers. Once he'd cashed in his back pay he'd head out. Somewhere down the line he'd trade the car, break the trail, and switch direction. He couldn't cut every link, at least not yet. He'd have to make some kind of contact arrangement with Vince. Even that made him nervous. But in the runup to the hearings there had to be some way for the prosecutors to reach him, and for him to respond.

He'd miss the dog, he'd realised. And therein lay another vulnerability. In movies they always started with the family pet.

Joe had followed him. He said, "Have you stopped to consider whether this will make any difference?"

"What do you mean?"

"Seems to me that if it's a revenge thing they could just show up and do the same damage whether you're here or not. Is this about keeping everyone safe, or is it an excuse to punish yourself? You did bad things, you told me that."

"Jesus, Dad."

"You're not coming back, are you?"

Danny had no immediate answer.

"If it's about us, don't go. We don't need that. And if it's about what you had to do, running off to live in a cave won't fix anything."

Danny said, "You don't know the half of it, Dad."

"Maybe I don't care."

For a moment Danny almost broke and confessed. But then he realised that it wasn't guilt over his handling of Rhianna Madisson that had pushed him to the edge. It was more the lack of it, the lack of any such remorse, that scared him.

Maybe Joe was right. Maybe he was running because he feared what he'd become.

THE NEXT THING YOU SEE WHEN YOU DIE

"You have to change the message on the voicemail," he said. "Take my name off there."

With resignation, Joe moved to the house phone. "You're rushing into this," he said. "Promise me you'll take some time to think it over."

The phone rang out just as he was about to touch it. He made a surprised face at Danny and picked up.

"Hello?"

Danny watched him, observed his father's puzzlement with a growing sense of disquiet.

"Hello? Who is this?"

He looked at Danny. "Sounds like someone crying," he said.

Danny moved at speed across the kitchen with his hand outstretched, and Joe gave up the phone. He watched as Danny listened. Danny heard sounds like a wind whistling through a strange landscape of tall rocky towers, but then a sob sold him that this was close-up breathing, pained and desperate.

He heard his name.

"Beth?" he said. "Is that you? What's happened?"

Danny

"Where are you?"

I don't know

There were noises off and the receiver at the far end was fumbled with, and then the nightmarish soundscape crashed down into a more commonplace reality with a man's voice.

The man said, "Do you know this woman? She's in my store. I don't know if she's drunk or high or what she is. I let her use the phone but if no one comes for her I'm calling 911."

"Is she hurt?"

"Her friend's weird and sketchy and I'm on my own here. I don't need this."

He gave an address. It was for a convenience store attached to a gas station out on the edge of town. Danny knew the area, it was where the airport freeway intersection and the suites motels were. The man sounded like someone whose patience was being tested.

Danny asked, "What friend? Who's she with?" but he'd hung up.

"Beth's hurt?" Joe said.

"I don't know," Danny said, heading for the door.

"Should I come?"

"Stay by the phone," Danny said.

22

THE SUITE MOTELS were like lit hives, business accommodation with grace notes of luxury, all life sealed away inside them in an empty floodlit park of concrete and cars all spread out like a tabletop model. There were two restaurants for travellers across the way, their interiors equally bright against the dying sunset, equally devoid of visible activity.

In the rushed drive out there Danny had been preoccupied by Beth's distress. He'd parked Joe's question at the back of his mind but now it had been asked, it would have to be faced.

What, really, was he proposing to run from?

The trust was real. And people died.

He'd done wrong in order to do good. He'd been asked to shoulder that weight, and now he was left with it. Guilt was as good a word as any. Just as his battered homeless victim had spent his last years ruthlessly erasing himself after the killing of a child, maybe Danny risked sliding into a similar spiral. Refusing a forgiveness that he didn't deserve. Not seeking inner peace, but fleeing from the very prospect of it.

The gas station was a pay-at-the-pump operation with no night window, but everything about the store signalled *open for business*. The forecourt was as empty and eerie as a piece of Edward Hopper art. He expected automatic doors to slide open as he approached, but nothing happened.

He didn't see a buzzer, so he banged on the window. No response. In this gathering darkness the interior shone out so bright that it almost hurt the eyes. Though the front wall was all glass, the view inside was restricted by the rows of shelving and the stacks of goods at their ends. He moved along, seeking out angles to see deeper.

Then he spotted something at the end of the store, a big curved mirror high in the corner. It would give the counter clerk a view down into the aisles. Danny was in the wrong place for a complete view but in the mirror he could see, for certain, the legs of someone lying on the floor part-hidden by a rack of phone accessories. The mirror's curve distorted the view, but from what he could make out it was a man's body.

Danny stepped away from the window. He took out his phone and called it in. He identified himself to the dispatcher and requested uniformed backup. Unless by some fluke there was a unit close to hand, that might take some time.

He went to the Buick and popped the trunk. Unlike newer models with their aerosol repair kits, the Buick carried a spare wheel and tire. Along with the spare came a tire iron. Joe had taught Danny how to change a wheel when he was fifteen. A skill that he had never had to use, nor now ever seemed likely to.

He took the iron over to the door and slid the flattened end into the space between the panel and the frame. He wasn't sure how the door had been jammed into place but he just threw in all the force he had. Nothing happened for several seconds but he kept up the pressure, and then suddenly it went with a bang. The door jumped in its frame and the glass split from side to side like cracking ice.

The glass didn't fall. He expected alarms. There were none. He worked the iron like a jemmy and forced the door open far enough for him to squeeze through.

He went straight to the fallen body. The night clerk he'd spoken to, at a guess. A youngish bearded man, hefty, soft rather than tough, with piercings and finger rings. He wore jeans and the maroon nylon jerkin of a store employee over a flannel shirt. He'd been dragged to this spot and there was a blood trail on the floor from a head injury but the man was breathing, noisily.

Beth had been right here, in something of a confused state, and she hadn't been here alone. There was the so-called weird and sketchy friend who may or may not have abandoned her.

Danny didn't like the sound of that. A friend. Yeah, right. There were some friends that good people needed rescuing from.

So where were they now? Beth had sounded drugged, or drunk, or worse.

The obvious conclusion was that Beth and the anonymous other had fled after whatever scene had played out with the man in the floor. There was a broken glass jar on the ground close by, thick glass, a likely weapon for his injuries. He couldn't imagine Beth clubbing a man to the ground. But someone had. So, again, concern.

The problem with the attack-and-flee scenario was that the entrance door had been jammed from the inside. The short blood trail suggested that the employee had been dragged just far enough to go unseen by anyone peering through the windows.

This had very much the feel of a setup.

A trap, even.

Imagined or not, Danny had a growing sense of another presence in the store. The only sound was the unconscious man's noisy breathing, and with a silent apology Danny reached out and pinched his nose shut for a few seconds to listen.

Nothing.

He couldn't see the security mirror from down here. When he let go the man on the floor resumed his breathing with an alarming snort, and Danny rose up again. Now he could see down the room. He got a good look at the mirror now, ceiling-mounted with its wide view of the entire store.

The image was like a miniature world, curving like the Earth. Nothing moved. Then something did.

In the corner of the fisheye view, almost about to disappear off the edge, he saw two distinct figures merged almost as one. They were on the floor by the chiller cabinets near the hardware aisle, huddled like a couple of orphans in a storm.

He started to move and suddenly he heard, "Danny, watch out!"

"Beth?"

And then a second voice: "Keep coming, Danny."

Rhianna.

Really?

THE NEXT THING YOU SEE WHEN YOU DIE

He came around into the aisle. They were at the far end of it. What he'd taken to be an embrace was anything but.

For a ghost, Rhianna was looking pretty solid. She had one arm around Beth, who had the miserable look of someone who'd been puking for an hour. They were both on the gray cement floor, backs against the wall. Rhianna's free hand held a box cutter to Beth's neck. Not the safety type but the heavy-duty kind with a large triangular blade, its sharp tip pushing into the soft flesh behind the jawbone and just under Beth's ear. Torn packaging for the knife lay on the floor beside them.

"What a great store," Rhianna said. "Everything you need. What's wrong with you, Danny? Didn't expect to see me?"

Danny did not. But there she was.

"I don't get it," Danny said.

"It's fate, Danny. We were being saved for this. We were neither of us meant to die yet."

"I mean, why here?"

"We stopped for gas. Your girlfriend was supposed to be under but she woke up. Found her way in and called you while I was in the restroom. So then I thought, okay. This must be the plan. You didn't make me wait too long. I appreciate that."

"Cops are coming."

"Real cops? We'll be done before they get here."

"If you want to punish me I'm right in front of you. You take it out on her, what happens? Nothing changes."

"Everything changes."

"The trial still goes ahead."

"I don't care about the trial, Danny. That life's over for me. It ended because of you. All I want now is for you to know how it feels."

"Like you with Nico, is that it?"

"Don't you even say his name!" She almost spat the words, and Beth winced away from her. The blade dug in and Beth made a sound.

To her Rhianna said, "Still, bitch." And then to Danny, "You can only dream of what we had. My soulmate. Then and now."

Danny reached for the only weapon he had.

The one he was sworn never to use.

He said, "There's something you ought to know, Rhianna. Your soulmate didn't die."

Blank. No response.

What he was telling her was true. People had died, and they returned in his nightmares. But Nico had never been one of them.

She might be hearing his words but their sense wasn't landing.

So Danny went on, "He's in a hotel under a fake name with a tag team of US Marshals for twenty-four-hour security. He's the prosecution's star witness."

"You're such a liar," she said. "Nice try. He found your cop phone and you killed him for it."

"Look at me, Rhianna." He began to move down the aisle. "I *am* a good liar, you know that. But take a long look and ask yourself, is he lying now? And did you ever ask the same of Nico? Because I have to tell you, he lied to you a lot."

Rhianna stared, her face set.

THE NEXT THING YOU SEE WHEN YOU DIE

"Fuck you and your tricks," she said.

"He stole the phone off me for insurance," Danny said. Closer now. "I couldn't get it back before they found it. Turning Nico was the outcome of six years' work for me. Hard work, twenty-four seven. The three who died, they're on my conscience. But Nico, no. He got a pretty sweet deal out of it. He's giving up the evidence and naming all the names."

"That's not my Nico."

Beth shifted a little in Rhianna's grip; the blade was still in place but it was almost as if Rhianna had forgotten her.

Danny said, "I'm sure he loved you in his way."

He was standing before her. He crouched down to her level and lowered his voice.

"But he gave you up with the rest of them."

That broke her. Beth was forgotten.

Screaming at Danny, Rhianna lunged.

Danny grabbed her, laying his hands on wherever he could, twisting her away from her captive. He felt a punch low in his gut as her knife met its target.

Despite her fury, she knew what she was doing. The blade was only short but she'd gone for the inside thigh, high up where the femoral artery lay close to the surface. Sever it and a person could bleed out in a couple of minutes. He clamped both of his hands over hers to keep her from twisting the blade, not knowing how much damage was already done. The two of them rocked together as she fought to kill him and he fought to stop her. His perception seemed to flicker but then he realised that it was the blue lights of an emergency vehicle, now outside. Backup was coming, maybe just a little too late.

Beth was scrambling up. Only halfway to her feet she started grabbing stuff from the shelves, pelting Rhianna with whatever came to hand. But this was the hardware section and it was mostly a rain of tape, aerosols, shin pads, work gloves…

Rhianna clung on, and Danny held her fast. Despite his efforts he could feel the blade move. The cops outside would be out there with weapons drawn and making their wary approach. Too slow, too slow.

Then Beth swung the pipe wrench.

Of the sales goods in the hardware section, it was the monster. It connected with Rhianna's head with a crack like a golf swing. Her head snapped to the side. Down below, the knife came out.

Out with the knife came blood. Lots of blood.

Rhianna was right out of it now. Beth started yelling.

Then the place was full of life and there were bodies moving all around. Danny sliding to the floor. Snatches of conversation that he couldn't follow. Beth telling someone, *I've got my thumb on the wound.* Medics shouldering through, someone tearing into his pants. One of them might even have been Rick, he couldn't say. Beth was crying again. To Danny it was all very distant, his consciousness draining with the bliss that comes with exhausted sleep.

This wasn't like the last time he'd died. That had been raw pain, a headlong plunge. This was something else. More subtle.

More dangerous.

THE NEXT THING YOU SEE WHEN YOU DIE

"Please, Danny," he heard Beth calling over the heads of the others as they crowded in and she was jostled to the back of the emergency crew. "Please. Don't you dare leave me again."

He fought to stay conscious but it was a losing battle. Then everything shifted around.

He was no longer in the store and he was aware that Beth was cradling his head now. Could be heaven. Could be the ambulance.

"Forgive me," he said.

What he wanted to hear was, Yes, Danny, you're forgiven.

Bur what he got from her was, "Live, you stupid fucker."

Okay, he thought.

Okay. I will.

Coda

NICO BECAME NICHOLAS, his past erased and replaced. New Social Security card, new number. The name change was legal, the court records sealed. While he traded dates and details for immunity they made him feel like a rock star, with hotels and room service and a rotating squad of bodyguards. After six weeks of TV and matchstick poker they moved him to a house deep in the country. The house stood within the fenced perimeter of a military base, although you'd never have known it. Between debriefings with Federal prosecutors he could roam outside in a limited way and with line-of-sight supervision, but that quickly palled.

When it came to the trial, he sailed through his evidence with no conscience. The one time his former boss caught his eye from the bulletproof glass dock, he responded to Armen's cold stare with a shrug.

With the passing of years the luster of stardom vanished along with the cash payment they'd fronted him. Sixty thousand; he'd expected more, and they cut it as soon as they got him into a job and paying his own rent. They'd told him he could choose his city but then shot down all his choices so in the end there he was, washing trucks for a transportation company in Olive Branch, Mississippi. Local law enforcement were told of his past, so apart from some hard drinking on weekends and a little dealing in weed there were few opportunities to misbehave.

One Saturday morning in April, just before ten, Nico woke with a raging headache after an unsatisfying Friday night in Silky O'Sullivan's, let down by friends who hadn't shown and buying drinks for indifferent women who stayed around just long enough to be polite. He'd driven home drunk and crashed face-down onto the covers in his one-bed one-bath second-floor rental. He lived alone. He was between girlfriends again. Women could find Nico charming, but he'd pretty much stopped trying.

When he turned out his pockets from the night before he couldn't find his car keys. Forgetting all else, he went out onto the deck and down the stairs. His Subaru was there but it was unsecured. He dived in and opened the glove box. The pawnshop handgun was missing. It was a legal weapon—no license or permit required, and thanks to the deal his record was clean—and given his history he liked to keep it close. He tried to think. Had he taken it up with him and blanked out the memory? It wouldn't be the first time.

He climbed the stairs back to his apartment. The door stood open. He went inside. He'd only been out for a couple of minutes but something had changed, and for a moment he struggled to work out what. All of the crap on his dining table had been swept

THE NEXT THING YOU SEE WHEN YOU DIE

onto the floor and now there was just a handful of new stuff in the middle of it. Well, not new. The small heap was a tangle of cheap baubles, neck chains and bracelets and at least one pair of earrings. Looking closer, he recognised some of them. Gifts he might once have given. He'd never been great with his gifts.

A knuckle of steel was pressed into the back of his neck, hard into the hollow at the base of his skull.

Behind him, someone spoke. He knew the voice.

"What we have here," she said, "is the harvest of your last seven years."

"Rhianna?" he said.

It was his last word.

But she cleared his headache.

Afterword:

Of Theft and Tribute

THERE'S AN OFT-QUOTED line from Albert Camus to the effect that each of us seeks to rediscover through art the essence of the images that first moved us. I beg the great man's forgiveness for lowering the tone, but I saw *Carnival of Souls* as the second feature in a Sunday horror double-bill at my local movie theater sometime around 1970 or '71 and this no-budget, hand-made horror from the 'sixties marked me for life.

I don't mean in a traumatic way, although I'm sure that a susceptible mind could find its combination of archetypal nightmare images and plain style genuinely disturbing. No: I was gripped by the way that it seemed to strike a succession of clear notes in my subconscious. It was like mainlining the essence of macabre. There's a misconception that horror in art is concerned with achieving disgust when in fact, done well, it produces a deep-reaching and peculiar form of delight.

Why am I telling you this now? Well, if you're both a reader and a certain kind of cinephile, there's an image in *The Next Thing You See When You Die* that may have caused a flicker of recognition.

Rest assured, I meant it.

The movie starts with a road race that ends in disaster, with a carload of friends running off a bridge and into the river. Alone from the water, in the first of the film's many memorable images, staggers Mary Henry, mud-splattered sole survivor of a mass drowning. Mary cleans up and goes on to take a job as a church organist in Salt Lake City. There she finds herself becoming steadily more detached from the world around her. When she's not playing the Devil's music or struggling to be noticed in an eerily silent town center, she's being haunted by a doleful apparition of a corpse-faced man. The apparition eventually leads her to a deserted lakeside pavilion where the dead waltz and welcome their own.

Whether it's Mary Henry in the Kansas River or Rhianna Madisson in Cooper Creek, drowning and transfiguration, whether real or symbolic, recur so often in myth and literature that they must be signalling some fundamental element within the human psyche. There's nothing so disturbing as a body of dark water. Few creatures so unsettling as those we thought lost there, who return.

The movie was released in 1962 and was made by a bunch of Kansas filmmakers with a background in corporate and industrial documentaries. Their output included such classics as *Signals— Read 'em or Weep* and (ahem) *To Touch a Child* (it's about education). Herk Harvey directed, John Clifford scripted. They raised money from local businesses and pressed friends and family into service

THE NEXT THING YOU SEE WHEN YOU DIE

both in front of and behind the camera. For their lead they hired Candace Hilligoss, a professional actress with a small handful of TV and B-movie credits, and struck lucky with her air of uninflected weirdness. Frankly, with someone more expensive the film might not have worked half so well.

In its making and in its achievement, I tend to think of it as a counterpoint to George Romero's *Night of the Living Dead*. Both were made outside the Hollywood system by people with a skill base in bread-and-butter, non-theatrical regional filmmaking. Both managed, by their very lack of conventional artifice, to strike directly at the viewer's unconscious. I regard *Carnival of Souls* as the Jung to *Living Dead*'s Freud.

Both films also had an equally rocky time in the marketplace, and left their makers similarly unrewarded. In my part of the UK, *Carnival* played that one night at my local fleapit and for many years never showed up on British TV. But boy, did it stay with me. *The Next Thing You See* is not a story of the supernatural. No ghosts, just haunted people. But my proposal is that it's from such hauntings our deep-wired sense of the supernatural has been formed.

So whether it's through Johnny Mays crashing off a dam (*Down River*), or Alina Petrovna's fierce attachment to her lakes homeland (*The Boat House*), or Rhianna, rising from the waters with her purpose reforged, I guess my own quest to reconnect with a moment of personal awakening continues.

This is not the greatest song in the world, no. This is just a tribute.

Novels by Stephen Gallagher
Chimera
Follower
Valley of Lights
Oktober
Down River
Rain
The Boat House
Nightmare, with Angel
Red, Red Robin
White Bizango
The Spirit Box
The Painted Bride

The Sebastian Becker Trilogy
The Kingdom of Bones
The Bedlam Detective
The Authentic William James

Novellas
In Gethsemane
Melody James
The Blackwood Oak

Collections
Out of His Mind
Plots and Misadventures
Comparative Anatomy: The Best of Stephen Gallagher

stephengallagher.com/books